# TRANSLATIONS

# —TRANSLATIONS—

## The Good Shepherd and Witness Coins

### Scott Spearing

RESOURCE *Publications* · Eugene, Oregon

Resource Publications
An Imprint of Wipf and Stock Publishers
199 W. 8th Ave., Suite 3
Eugene, OR 97401

www.wipfandstock.com

PAPERBACK ISBN: 978-1-7252-7985-8
HARDCOVER ISBN: 978-1-7252-7984-1
EBOOK ISBN: 978-1-7252-7986-5

02/19/2021

For Mom and Dad

# CONTENTS

—Book 1—
## THE GOOD SHEPHERD • 1

Chapter 1 • 3

Chapter 2 • 6

Chapter 3 • 10

Chapter 4 • 13

Chapter 5 • 15

Chapter 6 • 19

Chapter 7 • 24

Chapter 8 • 28

Chapter 9 • 31

Chapter 10 • 36

Chapter 11 • 40

—Book 2—
## WITNESS COINS • 43

Chapter 1 • 45

Chapter 2 • 48

Chapter 3 • 55

Chapter 4 • 66

Chapter 5 • 75

Chapter 6 • 81

Chapter 7 • 91

Chapter 8 • 96

Chapter 9 • 108

Chapter 10 • 115

Chapter 11 • 119

Chapter 12 • 126

Chapter 13 • 130

Chapter 14 • 139

Chapter 15 • 146

Chapter 16 • 152

Chapter 17 • 158

Epilogue • 168

—Book 1—

# THE GOOD SHEPHERD

# CHAPTER 1

It was a bright and crisp late autumn day as the last of the leaves sailed from their summer harbors for distant shores on the cool breeze. The old bell in the seminary's bell tower tolled the third hour of the afternoon. Most of the students were in their studies and classrooms as the third strike of the hour echoed through the ancient campus of St. Peter's Seminary. All except the graduating seniors, who were huddled together in the hallways of the main administration hall. Here may have been the only place on campus that was not feeling the coolness of the approaching winter.

The dozen and a half young men were discussing, in excited but hushed voices, the possibilities of their first assignments into their chosen lives. Discussions were centered on who would be assigned to one of the great cathedrals with their massive gothic structures, the awe-inspiring stained glass windows, and sacred relics, and the sermons; yes, those empowering sermons to the masses, all of those poor, ignorant souls who will need to hear the words for comfort, guidance, and condemnation for their sinful ways. These were the thoughts of the hour; for within the hour, each student would know his destination to come in the next two weeks. Occasionally, a snicker or chuckle could be detected here and there when those in the group would conjecture as to who would be going to some of the poorer parishes. There had even been a rumor that a small parish in the coal-mining towns of the Blue Ridge Mountains was in need of assistance. It was even said that the presiding priest had to hold services in cowsheds and taverns in various villages because there were no proper churches to hold services. And the largest of these hamlets, Bethell, boasted a wooden church large enough to hold the whole town of one hundred and eighty-five people, provided that the local livestock were not in need of its shelter.

Then the room fell silent. A determined set of footsteps pounded across the hall to the community board. Not a soul moved as this thin specter pinned a piece of paper to the board. The person turned and paused, scanning the room from one group to the next; as his stare focused on each group, their heads wilted from his gaze. Then the footsteps rhythmically advanced back across the hall. The vacuum left by the specter at the community board was quickly filled. Whispers were punctuated with brief phrases of thanks and praises as each candidate located his name on the list and discovered his destination for the next two years. Suddenly, there was a parting of the collection as Matthew Brooks, top of his class, tall and with a notable presence, waded up to the board. Mr. Books had shown to be exceedingly knowledgeable in both Old and New Testament and could recite any one of the one hundred and five Psalms from memory; it also had been said that he was only one of three who had ever been able to single-handedly lift the large stone covering the access to the seminary's dilapidated cistern. This feat was performed one stormy day when one of the roof drains had plugged and threatened to flood the kitchen if the blockage was not removed. A bird's nest was the cause of the mayhem right where the pipe entered the cistern.

All fell deftly quiet as a single "no" was uttered from the imposing figure. Matthew turned in a daze. Then a flame grew in his eyes and his posture stiffened. The small puddle that Matthew had waded through to the community board now parted as the Red Sea had done before Moses. Matthew marched off with a measured stride through the gap and down the hall to first corridor on the left. Matthew had no more than turned the corner when all attentions returned to the board, but this time they were not looking for their name but the name of Matthew Brooks. And there across from his name was simply penned Bethell.

The door flew open as Matthew stormed into the head monsignor's office. Father Griffith was seated at his desk with Father Downier standing to his left. Father Downier jumped as the doors flew open and then quickly regained his composure, the one with a disapproving gaze that could turn a boiling pot of water to ice. Father Griffith continued his inspection of the paperwork before him. After all of these years, the seasoned head of the school was not easily startled. With a slow and deliberate movement, Griffith placed the document down on the desk and gazed up at the now red-faced Brooks. Griffith removed the wire frame glasses from his prominent nose and simply said, "Yes, my son?"

Matthew was almost speechless from his anger at the lowly appointment and from the unchallenging tone of his prey. "Wh . . . Why! What have I done to deserve this . . . this Bethell?" Matthew's voice started as an old fireplace bellows and rose to the roar of a young lion. "I have the highest marks, I know passages by memory that most need to search for, and I can debate Satan into a box."

With that, Father Downier gasped and roared back in a more elderly lion tone, "How dare you! You barge in unannounced, question the Father's decisions, and now you boast to take on—"

But Father Downier was cut short, and Matthew's welling rebuttal was stayed by the simple gesture of Father Griffith's raised right hand. "Matthew, you were chosen," Father Griffith began in his soft but firm tone that demanded one to listen or a word may be missed, "because of your accomplishments and knowledge. You see, Father Gates of the Bethell parish broke his leg and is unable to travel to the different communities in his parish. He has a dozen hamlets nestled in the folds of the mountain that depend on his biweekly visits. Father Gates's age has not helped the healing of his leg, and he can no longer traverse his parish as he has done for the last thirty-seven years. You, my son, have been chosen to assist Gates, and no other will do." When Matthew heard thirty-seven years and thought this was to be his tenure, or longer, the rage and wind that had filled his sails faded into disillusion.

The only word Matthew could utter was "but," and Father Griffith continued.

"You must be at your best and prepare for the journey to Bethell. The train leaves in a few days so pack what you need and see to the warm clothing. With winter coming, the mountains will feel the cold first and the weather can be trying. Go see Father Neuson for proper attire and your travel arrangements. Now, go with God." With that, Matthew felt he was in a dream, in his case a nightmare. He found himself quietly walking through the open door and reverently closing them as he passed.

With the click of the door, Father Downier erupted in a stream of disgust and contempt for the way that Matthew had acted. He even suggested and almost demanded that the student be ejected from the school without graduation. Again, Father Griffith raised his hand, stifling Downier's rage. And in words almost inaudible, Griffith spoke to where Matthew had stood, "It is what is needed . . . for all concerned. I only hope this works because I don't know how it will work. But I pray it will."

# CHAPTER 2

Days later, Matthew was gazing at the passing countryside as the train ushered him from one station to the next. With each passing moment, the countryside seemed to change, growing older, more primitive. Cows and goats seemed to be the spectators to Matthew's journey into his perceived exile. Ever since that afternoon when he learned of his destination, Matthew started to collapse inwardly. He shunned many of the optional end-of-semester ceremonies and only attended the few mandated by his superiors.

And constantly, there was the nagging question of *Why me? . . . Bethell, Bethell of all places! What did I do wrong? Who did I wrong? Why am I being punished?*

As the train continued its laborious trek up the side of one of many mountains, the momentum slowed and so did the rocking motion of each car. Matthew laid his head against the window, still staring at the hazy mountains with their misty valleys. Since the posting of the assignments, Matthew had only slept a few hours each night. Those few hours he did sleep were restless, and each time he awoke, the question laid before him was "Why me?" As the coach swayed, Matthew's mind drifted back to his earlier days at St. Francis's where he grew up.

The nuns ruled the children with an iron hand and punishment was swift and deliberate. There was little love to be shared between the nuns and their charges. There were so few to care for so many. But there was always something to eat, even though it was the same thing day after day and usually week after week. Every once in a while, a local farmer or merchant would drop off a sack of turnips or a side of meat. The meat when available was usually old smelling and came with a collection of flies and other passengers, which had to be scrapped off prior to any further preparation in the kitchen. The rest of the time, the older children with the nuns would work in St. Francis's garden, consisting of mainly potatoes, tomatoes, squash, and various herbs. Everything else was gathered in a local wooded area.

Clothing was another matter. Bundles of discarded clothes were occasionally dropped at the doorstep. These usually smelled of dampness and mold. Several of the younger girls would be put in charge of sorting through the clothes—most of the time the term "rags" was a better description—into piles of items for daily wear, items for nightwear, and items which had no purpose within the walls of this establishment, as one of the sisters would proclaim while removing the offensive pile to the burn pit behind the kitchen. The remaining clothes were then distributed to those who were in the most need of that particular item. Again, one of the sisters would make distribution just before bedtime and before their nightly prayers. The next morning would be their first opportunity to try on their new garments. Of course, size was never a prerequisite of ownership. Many a time one would be lost in the shirt or trousers. The sisters would always tell them to count their blessings and that it was something to grow into. On the occasion when the item was too small, they would try to trade with one of the younger children when the sisters were not looking.

This made Matthew cringe seeing how he was a little tall for his age and was constantly bartering for some item a bit larger. He could bully a smaller child into making a trade, but more often than not, the sisters would find out about how the transaction occurred. And the nuns' retributions were swift and severe with little to no appeal from the accused prior to the punishment. But if one did try to protest his fate, the punishment would be increased to levels greater than what the original offense required. And yet there were good memories, mainly pertaining to the lessons. Matthew had literally lost himself in the stories of the Bible. He could see himself as David slaying Goliath; or Solomon the Wise handing down a decision between two bickering subjects; or Joshua marching around the fortress of Jericho and watching the walls falling down. He was there. He could see it, smell it, and hear it. All of this so far away from St. Francis's and its daily drudge of cleaning, gardening, and sorting.

Then another thought came to Matthew, a memory of such clarity that it seemed to only have happened yesterday. He was about ten, and it was after one of those long, trying days where he seemed to be working off one punishment after another. He was in bed in the boys' dorm about to go to sleep when two of the sisters entered for the regular nightly bed check. He acted as though he was asleep but listened to the sisters' hushed conversation.

"That one has been a handful today," remarked one sister, motioning to Matthew. "He has been into everything. I had to give him four separate tasks to perform before the dinner hour and one following."

The other sister remarked, "It's just the age. He seems to do well in his lessons."

"That may be, but this one will follow the hands of the devil . . . I can tell," replied the first. "He's always been a handful, and it will get worst with age."

The second sister added, "I don't suppose he can help it with the start that he had, finding him in that basket on the doorstep of this orphanage."

The first sister interjected, "I heard that they found a woman the next day, drowned down by the bridge, a prostitute that had been run out of town. I have a feeling it was his mother."

"But the father," added the second, "the father, I'm almost certain that he was the thief and robber they caught and hung only a few days after they found his mother in the river. Look at him, don't you notice the resemblance?"

"Yes, now that you mention it, I do. And with stock like that, what more would you expect from the little heathen?" said the first, somberly.

"Well, it's in God's hands now, but such a child usually comes to no good," said the second, echoing the other sister's demeanor.

That was it! Matthew's head bounced from the window as the coach made an abrupt swing on the tracks. Matthew thought it was all so clear now—he had the wrong parents. It was not his fault but his parents'. And now, he was receiving their punishment. After all of his years of struggle to better himself, to be the best, and to show his worth, it was all for naught. He was marked for life to never truly succeed but to always miss the goal he had set his sights on, a grand cathedral—the massive stone structures with their ornate carvings, the frail but beautifully awe-inspiring stained glass windows, and the richly ornate ceremonies performed for the hundreds, no thousands, of sinners who could only dream of the meanings of the services as spoken to God in the rituals. Matthew's mind was swimming in a torrent of thoughts and ideas. Confusion seemed to have pulled back its veil and allowed Matthew to see, for the first time, why he was heading to Bethell.

At that moment, a small structure was visible in the bend of the track up ahead. As the train coasted and slowed its tiresome journey on the seemingly never-ending rails, Matthew read the sign on the little train station, "Bethell." The sign was so old and worn, the lettering was a little hard to read—so much so that the "t" was almost nonexistent.

A small grimace tried to creep to Matthew's lips as he thought that a missing "t" made the sign a little more appropriate.

CHAPTER 3

Matthew quickly gathered a small suitcase and a stack of books wrapped in brown paper for the trip. Prior to leaving St. Peter's, Matthew was given a traveling cloak and a pair of gloves. He figured that the cloak was a one-size-fits-all type of garment and was given to him since he was going to no major city were fashion would have dictated a well-fitted coat. Here again, he felt that he would just have to make do. There were pockets on the inside of the cloak where he had earlier placed the gloves and where he had placed a small traveling Bible. With his suitcase and books, Matthew prepared to step off of the train and into his not-so-grand assignment of Bethell.

The cool, brisk mountain air washed over Matthew as he prepared to step onto the wooden box that had been placed at the end of the car's steps. The warmth of the railcar was quickly brushed away as a sudden gust washed over the station platform. Matthew wrapped the traveling cloak a little tighter, trying to capture and hold a little of the warmth. Matthew noticed a group of men at the far end of the platform unloading boxes and barrels from one of the freight cars with amazing precision. At the same time, a small pile of packages and a mail pouch were lifted from the wooden platform and hoisted into the freight car that had once housed the mound of boxes and barrels on the platform. With the last of the packages retrieved, the men disappeared back onto the train.

Suddenly from behind, Matthew heard, "You . . . Stop . . . No, stop!" As Matthew turned to see the source of commands, something small plowed into his legs. The small creature was about three feet tall and was comprised of ratty clothes of one form or another and covered in coal dust and dirt. The urchin bounced back and landed on its bottom. A surprised look was on the child's face as well on Matthew's. Before Matthew could blink the little critter sprang up, passed around him, and scurried off in the direction of the newly delivered freight on the platform. Now a new sound of hollow footsteps pounding on the wooden planks approached Matthew.

The source was the overweight station master, Mr. Haddor. "What, what are you doing? Couldn't you have grabbed the little retch?" puffed Haddor. With Haddor's next inhalation the train's engine announced its departure with a blast of its whistle. Grunting, creaking, clanking, and other shifting sounds erupted from the cars next to the two individuals on the platform.

The little one had disappeared among the freshly delivered boxes and crates. As the train's caboose clattered down the track in its endless chase to catch the engine, the station master checked his pocket watch and returned it to his vest pocket. "Now sir—" Haddor stopped short, noticing Matthew's attire and realizing that the only scheduled passenger for the day, for the week, and for the last month was to be one Matthew Brooks, Father Gates's new assistant.

Haddor stammered out an apology, "I . . . I'm sorry, good sir, I didn't realize it was you. Please accept my apology. I . . . I get so frustrated chasing these little kids around the station. This is no place for the little urchins. They get into the freight and heaven help if one should fall under the wheels! Can you imagine the paperwork and reports I would have to fill out?"

Matthew inquired, "What of the child's parents; can't they maintain some discipline?"

"It was one of the town's orphans that Father Gates has tried to watch over. He tries to do so much in Bethell and in the other villages. But with the mining accidents and illnesses in the winters Father Gates seems to be gathering more and more of these little waifs," Haddon explained.

"How many are in the orphanage?" Matthew inquired.

Haddon puffed. "Oh, it's five or six from what I understand. It's rather hard to keep up with such things. Oh dear, look at that. The little retch has soiled your coat with coal dust."

Matthew looked down and attempted to brush away the dirt and soot with little avail. "I've only been traveling for four days, and this is how I'm greeted." Matthew was becoming irritated. "I understood that a Mr. Felder was to meet me and provide transportation to . . . Bethell." The word almost became stuck in his throat. "I only see you here, even the waif has disappeared. What am I to do!" Matthew's irritation was rising and starting to show on his face. At this point, only the coldest gust from down the tracks would have been able to cool his disposition.

The station master responded, "Pappy, um . . . Mr. Felder, he's had a problem with his wagon, but he should be here in an hour or two," as he fumbled at his pocket watch.

"What!" exclaimed Matthew.

Haddon jumped in, "Pappy had to get one of the wheels replaced. He should be on his way here now to collect you and your things." Matthew briskly walked over to and around to the far side of the station house. The rhythmic pounding of his lengthy steps on the wooden flooring was only broken by the shuffling sound of the station master's feet closely behind Matthew.

As Matthew stood surveying the dusty road that passed in front of the station, he absentmindedly started to brush at his traveling cloak. "Which way to Bethell . . . and how far?" Matthew glared.

"Well, you see," started the station master, "the town is about eight miles that way," pointing to the left.

Matthew's head dropped to his chest. "Is that the only way to town?"

"There is the walking path." Haddon was pointing to a narrow division in the woods just across the dirt road. "Bethell is only four and a half miles by the path. It's fairly well-marked but not too flat. Several hills and a couple of dried creek beds must be crossed before you come to the town," offered Haddon.

"How long before nightfall?" questioned Matthew.

Haddon fumbled for his watch and responded, "A good four hours, I'd say." Matthew stood there motionless weighing his options. Then with a sudden shift, Matthew started across the road, heading for the path. Haddon called out, "What should I tell Pappy?"

Matthew replied over his shoulder, "Tell him I'll see him in Bethell and have him bring my books and suitcase to the church. I'll be waiting for my things."

With that, Matthew, without hesitation, marched into the narrow gap in the brush. With his disappearance into the woods, the station master shook his head and busied himself back around to the station house.

# CHAPTER 4

It felt good to be stretching his legs after the long train ride and sitting in one station after another. The wood's canopy was bare for the most part; very few leaves clung to their summer residence. They now lay in a multicolored carpet across the forest floor. Even with the leafy covering, the path was still very visible. Occasionally, Matthew's passing would startle a squirrel or a rabbit, sending the small creatures scurrying for a nearby tree or another pile of leaves. As he walked, his brooding became difficult in the setting he was traversing. There was peacefulness in this place, even with the crunching of dried leaves and dead twigs. Great, billowy clouds would pass over, casting shadows in the woods, creating a contrast of stark bare wooded sentries and the multicolor carpet as the rays of sunlight broke through.

At one point, Matthew stopped at a dried streambed to look down the opening in the trees to see a small shallow valley. And there, off to the right, appeared to be a small brown ribbon winding its way next to the dried bed. That must be part of the road that his belongings would be traveling, he thought to himself. Before continuing up the dried stream bed embankment, Matthew noticed a long stick that must have washed down the stream earlier in the year. Matthew picked it up and examined it with some curiosity. It was nearly as long as he was tall and was void of any branches or twigs. He did notice that it had a slight twist two thirds of the way down below his hand. But the diameter of the stick filled his hand comfortably and seemed to make a good companion for the remainder of his hike.

With this, Matthew pressed on with a little less heavy heart. Even though the way was not overly exerting, Matthew was getting tired. Not resting well for the past several weeks and the four days of travel were catching up with him. Matthew came up on a slight rise where several large boulders protruded from the earth. The path wound in among them and back off into the trees. Matthew stopped and looked at the sky and tried to judge the time by the height of the sun off of the hills. "I must have at least another two hours, and I should be two thirds to three quarters of the way there by now," he mused to himself. "A short rest wouldn't hurt; I have plenty of time."

Selecting a smaller boulder that was about three feet in diameter and height, Matthew settled himself down against the rock in the sun. He adjusted his walking partner next to himself and pulled the travel cloak up around his legs and across his chest. The warmth of the sun and the stillness of the boulder field were the conditions that sleep required to lull a weary traveler into a much-needed rest.

# CHAPTER 5

A sound. A sound of a child crying was what Matthew was first aware of even before his eyes were open. But as he opened his eyes, the surroundings had changed. He was staring at a bright, bleak, rocky landscape—a few patches of scrubby bushes off to the left, a couple of scraggily twigs that might be called trees in front, and a rocky slope rising off to the right. And the heat, the heat was shimmering off of the rocks and dirt. This had to be a dream, but it felt so real. And there was still the sound of a child crying, somewhere in one of those scrubby bushes.

Just when Matthew thought this dream could not become any stranger, he was awakened by, "Get up, get up. You've been sleeping again. What have I told you about sleeping on your watch? Get up! One of the lambs is in trouble." A hand extended from the voice, grabbed Matthew by the shoulder, and hoisted him to his feet.

Matthew spun to witness a partially shrouded specter, close to six feet tall. He was tall but thin with a long beard with hints of grey strung through the dark-brown mass. He was clothed in layers of off-white and brown coarse-woven robes. With his left hand on Matthew's shoulder, his right hand, weathered but strong, grasped a long pole with a crook on the top. Matthew tried to wrench himself from this stranger's grasp but was unable to free himself. This should have been a simple feat due to Matthew's size and physique. Then it struck Matthew like a ton of bricks; he was small, not quite five feet tall. And the hands that were struggling with the stranger's arm were dark and small. He stopped struggling and stared in amazement at his hands.

"Malich . . . Malich is everything all right?" Another robed individual called out to the stranger holding Matthew's shoulder. The second stranger came scrambling over the rocky slope. "The way that lamb is crying, I thought the big cat or a bear was attacking it," said the second, slightly shorter man. He too was dressed in a similar style and color of attire and carrying a staff with a crooked T-shaped hook on the top.

"It's all right Narrac, the boy fell asleep on watch again, and one of the lambs has wandered in to the briers. I think Matthew is about to learn a very pointed lesson about sheep," Malich said looking down at Matthew.

Narrac started to sit down on one of the rocks. "This should be interesting to watch."

But Malich waved him off. "Go on back to your flock; you don't want to set a bad example for our small friend." With that, Narrac picked himself up and picked his way back over the rocky hill.

Matthew was still awestruck and confused more than ever. And that crying, it seemed louder and grating on the nerves like chalk on a . . . he could not remember the thing you write on with chalk. It was there on the tip of his tongue, but at the same time, his mind seemed blank, no memory of what the chalk was for.

"Matthew," Malich began as he started to guide the boy toward one of the small bushes making all of the noise. "When you don't watch the sheep, they tend to wander off into the quickest trouble they can find. Your lamb that you're in charge of has found a brier bush. Since he is your responsibility, you have to save him from his mess that he has created. He has been calling and calling, and I don't want him attracting a predator to the flock. Now get in there and pull him out." Malich released his grip on Matthew, who just stood there bewildered.

Matthew felt his arms and hands starting to reach toward the brier bush as though they had a mind of their own. The lamb had wrapped itself from all sides with the bush during its struggle to free itself. The more the lamb pulled and shifted, the more the barbed twigs entangled with the lamb's short, fleecy wool. As Matthew gingerly reached in to grab the lamb by some wool on its hind quarters, the struggling lamb shifted causing the sharp thorns to scrape Matthew's hand and wrist.

"Ouch!" He drew back his hand and caught another thorn on the way out. A few little droplets of blood squeezed their way to the surface of the back of his hand. "I can't reach him. He's too deep in to the thorns," he said rubbing his hand.

"Matthew, where is the staff I gave you? Have you lost this one also?" Malich said as he looked back to where the boy had been sleeping.

By some reflex, Matthew scurried over and found the hiking stick he had picked up earlier when, again, there was the blank place in his mind.

As though he knew what he had been doing when he first acquired the stick but as if it were a dream. And the stick was larger than what he remembered, bigger around and longer. Matthew stood in amazement once again with the stick in hand but did not understand why.

Malich slightly shook his head and then gazed upward. "What shall I do with this little lamb?" Then he reached forward and took the walking stick from Matthew and replaced the stick with his shepherd's crook. Matthew stared at the crook of the staff as it hung over his head. Although crudely hewn there was a certain grace and balance to the way the wood twisted its way into a hook. The shepherd's tool also seemed to better fit his smaller hands. "Matthew, your lamb is becoming less patient and more tangled," reminded Malich. "How will you free the lamb?"

Matthew thought for a moment, and then moved toward the lamb, taking the shepherds crook and tried to hook the lamb's hind quarter. After snaking the crook through the brier, Matthew was able catch the lamb, but that is all he could do. No matter how hard he pulled, the lamb did not move from the thorn bush, and the lamb hollered even louder, which Matthew thought would be impossible from such a small creature.

Finally, Malich intervened more on behalf of the lamb and the concern of the noise it was making. "Matthew, stop! You are getting nowhere. Release the lamb and come around to the other side of the bush with your staff." As Matthew circled the bush, he saw that the lamb was actually starting to protrude on the far side of the bush. "Now, take the crook of the staff, lay it flat against the side of the lamb's neck and slide it down his side. This will pull the briers out of his fleece," Malich instructed.

At first, the briers resisted but then gradually gave way to the prompting of the crook. After repeatedly rubbing the sides of the lamb with the crook, the lamb calmed down and was able to move a little farther out of the bush.

"Now," continued Malich, "put you staff down, grab the lamb's fleece at the shoulders, and pull him out."

Matthew reached over and handed the staff to Malich, carefully reached in, grabbed two handfuls of wool, and pulled. After a few good, hardy pulls, the lamb came free and ended up on top of Matthew who landed on his backside. By this time, the lamb was so tired from its ordeal in the brier bush it could hardly stand.

Malich, leaning on the shepherd's crook, smiled at Mathew's new predicament. Matthew realized that he too was a little tired from all of the work and decided to rest a minute with the lamb in his lap. "You see,"

Malich says, "many a times the only way to get through a tough situation is to push on through, the way you were originally heading. When stuck, all of the thrashing and complaining only make the situation worse. A little patience and a lot of persistence will get one through the situation." With that, Malich reached down with his free hand and lifted the lamb, cradling it in his arm.

As Matthew stood up, Malich handed the crook back to Matthew. "Come on, we need to get back to the rest of the flock." Malich motioned with his head. As they walked back around the bush toward the rocky ridge, Malich remarked, "I don't think this little one will be getting into any trouble any time soon. I think he'll be more than happy to stay with his mother for a while. But I think you need to keep a special watch on this one. As a matter of fact, I think you both can learn from each other. So, he's yours to protect and watch over." Matthew followed Malich back over the ridge.

# CHAPTER 6

There before them were some forty to fifty sheep grazing on the sparse vegetation. A few started to move off from the rest of the flock. Malich started to call out but stopped when Narrac came from around a rock outcropping in front of the direction the sheep were heading.

"I've got them. They were working this way for some time. I thought I would head them off before they went too far." With that, Narrac started waving his arms and made a huffing sound. The sheep acted more like someone who had been caught doing something they knew they were not supposed to be doing. They turned and halfheartedly trotted back to the herd.

Malich walked straight over to one of the ewes with the lamb. "Mother, I believe this belongs to you." He laid the lamb next to her. The ewe bleated twice as though scolding the wayward lamb and thanking Malich. Malich turned to Matthew and said, "This looks like a good spot for you to watch over the sheep."

"But where are you going?" Matthew inquired.

"Narrac and I are going up over the next ridge, over there. We need to find a new grazing area. The sheep have just about stripped this place of food. We also need to find a source of water. I think they are starting to get thirsty. That's why I think that small group was starting to wander off before Narrac stopped them. I seem to remember a small stream not far from here." Matthew must have looked panic-stricken. Malich said, "It will be all right, we won't be gone for long or that far away."

Matthew looked at the flock. "But what if they start to run off in different directions?"

Malich looked over the sheep. "Just remember what I've told you. Sheep will only scatter if they think they are in danger. If a few start to stray from the main flock, move over in front of them, talk to them softly, and shoo them back to the flock. Loud sudden noises make them think there is danger, and they will blindly start running about. You also need to watch out for predators. They will try to scatter the flock and pick off a straggler or one of the lambs. You think you can do this?"

Matthew nodded his head.

"Good," Malich said as he waved at Narrac and then pointed at a cleft between two outcroppings and started to walk in that direction. Matthew watched as the two men met and started walking to the cleft.

Narrac stopped and seemed to be questioning Malich while pointing back to the flock and Matthew. Malich calmly placed his hand on Narrac's shoulder and started to steer him through the cleft. Then they were gone. Matthew surveyed the flock. All was quiet with most of the sheep lying down. It was the heat of the day, so who would want to be moving around. Most of the sheep had found some shade in the shadows of the outcroppings, while others found shade under a scraggly, wilted looking fig tree.

Matthew started to grow bored and noticed the crook he was resting on. He noticed a few knots and nicks along the vertical shaft of the crook. The bottom end was well worn and chipped. Moving up to the hooked portion of the crook, Matthew noticed several scratches in the wood. He figured that these came from the briar bush where he and Malich had pulled the lamb.

Just then, he noticed a shadow passing over the crook. Matthew looked up and was blinded for a moment by the midday sun. He held up his hand to block the burning orb. There, off to his right he saw the owner of the shadow, a great hawk. Matthew looked down and then over to the flock. The hawk did not seem to be interested in the flock by the outcroppings or those by the fig tree. It was circling over by a small pile of stones. Matthew shifted his position and saw the ewe and her lamb, his lamb. The ewe was lying by the pile of stones while the lamb, not more than the length of the crook away, was chewing on a bit of vegetation.

Matthew felt a cold chill reached up and grabbed him. "What am I to do? The hawk was about to drop down on the unsuspecting lamb. If I shout at the hawk and throw stones at it, the sheep might panic and start to scatter. If I don't do anything, the lamb will be lost. What should I do?"

Matthew thought, *Lord what should I do? I'm to protect the lamb, and I don't know what to do. Anything I can think of will make matters worse.*

Then, as though Matthew knew what he was doing, he started walking straight toward the ewe and lamb. As he drew closer, the ewe saw him approaching and started to stir as though to get up. The lamb had not taken notice. Matthew calmly started to speak to the ewe in a soft low voice. "It's okay mama, I'm the one who helped bring your lamb back. Just stay right there, and everything will be all right." The ewe bleated softly and watched Matthew. Standing in between the ewe and the lamb, Matthew raised the crook over his head in both hands and started to rotate the crook back and forth. The lamb looked up at Matthew and moved over to his right side. "It's okay little one, stay right here, and the hawk will not harm you."

After a short time, this action discouraged the hawk, and it flew off in search of an easier prey. Matthew was thankful because his arms were starting to get tired. As he saw the hawk fly off, he lowered the crook. He then noticed that the lamb had laid down right next to his foot. Matthew knelt down and started to scratch the lamb on the head between its ears. "It's all right. You did just fine. Now stay near your mother and—"

Just then, Matthew felt a push from behind that sent him sprawling. He started to scramble to see his attacker and rolled over to a sitting position. There was the ewe standing next to the lamb. The ewe bleated at Matthew and started to nudge the lamb to get up. The pair then wandered over to the group under the fig tree. Matthew sat in awe to this event.

"That's gratitude for you." Matthew jumped to his feet and spun around. There stood Malich and Narrac grinning from ear to ear. Narrac continued, "Not bad, not bad at all. There is some wisdom in you after all." Turning to Malich, Narrac continued, "I'll go and collect our supplies and meet you two by the cleft." With that, Narrac moved off toward the outcropping.

"We were heading back when we saw the hawk circling. We saw everything you did from the cleft. Did you know that the hawk might still attack?" Malich inquired.

"No, I didn't think about that. But why would the hawk still attack?" pondered Matthew.

"If the hawk is needing to feed its young, it would have made several attempts to drive you away to get to that lamb. But you stood there waving the crook over your head. How did you know what to do and at the same time not frighten the flock?" questioned Malich.

Matthew stood there and just shrugged his shoulders like any young lad and then said, "I just asked God what to do. Then I just knew what to do, and I wasn't afraid." As he said this, he realized that he was not afraid although one would think that he should have been.

At about that time, Narrac came back with several bundles slung over his shoulder. The bundles were wrapped in the same type of material that the shepherds' coats were made of. Narrac unslung the bundles and handed one of them to Malich and then turned to Matthew and presented him a bundle. Matthew stared at it then slowly reached for it. "You better take it," Narrac offered.

"It will be cold again tonight, and you do want to eat your dinner?" Malich added, "One or two more nights of dried figs and bread, then we'll be able to see what my wife has made for us. She's to meet us by the town's gate before the Sabbath. I think there might be something special prepared for us."

Narrac asked, "What's the occasion?"

Malich replied, "Remember the caravan we saw a little while ago? It was from Jerusalem. My wife's sister tries to send her something different every chance she gets. Sometimes its herbs, sometimes cloth, and other times incense or perfume."

Narrac snorted, "Incense and perfume, I take it your sister-in-law is not overly fond of our profession."

"Ah yes. We can't all be merchants or tradesmen," remarked Matthew.

"Yes, but herding sheep is good, honest work," retorted Narrac. "People don't realize how dangerous and difficult it is trying to keep these critters alive. Besides, if we didn't tend to the flocks, what would all of those town and city dwellers eat and keep themselves warm with on cold nights?"

Malich shouldered his bundle. "As in nature and with God's will, we all have our parts to play, one no more important than the other. Just like the body, the eyes can see, the ears hear, and the nose smell, but the feet would not know where to step or which way to run on their own. They need the eyes to see where they are stepping and the ears to hear someone calling them, and—"

Matthew piped in, "Or a nose to tell them which way their dinner awaits?"

"Very good," both elders echoed. Narrac lifted his bundle. "I think someone is starting to get hungry."

"Well, we have to move the sheep to the new grazing space and get them sheltered before we can eat. There is only a few more hours before the sun starts to set," said Malich. "Narrac, if you'll take the back-left side of the flock, and Matthew, you take the back-right side. I'll start leading the sheep through the cleft."

Without another word, the two moved to their positions, flanking the flock. Malich watched as the two took their positions and then started to stroll toward the middle of the flock. In a calm, almost melodic tone, he started talking to the sheep. "Up, up the day is not done. We go to greener pastures and sweet cool waters. Come, come it's time to go. Safe is the way for ram and ewe. Follow, follow for now we move." And with that Malich walked straight for the cleft in the rocks. The sheep closest to Malich started to follow as though they were on a leash. And as those followed, other seemed to drift toward the void created by the sheep that followed Malich.

Narrac nudged a couple of sheep that were still lying in the shadow of the rocks saying, "Up, up, move." And with the prodding, they gathered themselves up and walked to follow the rest.

Matthew, at the same time, found the ewe and the lamb by the fig tree still lying there even though the others had drifted off to follow the procession. "Come on, mama; it's time for you and the little one to move on. You don't want to be left behind. Besides, the hawk may come back."

With that the ewe snorted at Matthew, turned, and trotted toward the back of the flock. But the lamb stood there and started to bleat at Matthew as though to make some point. Then the lamb turned and realized that the ewe had already left. It took off bleating after its mother, catching her just before passing into the cleft. Narrac and Matthew stood there laughing, and then they too passed through the cleft to follow the sheep.

# CHAPTER 7

While following the sheep, Matthew and Narrac had little to do except for the occasional prodding with the crook of a sheep that was distracted by a stray outcropping of grass. Matthew asked, "Why do the sheep follow Malich? He didn't yell and scream at them; he quietly called to them and then started walking off. They all started following."

Narrac smiled. "You see, the sheep have learned to trust Malich. He protects them, leads them to where there is food and fresh water. Haven't you noticed when the sheep are uneasy or seem nervous, Malich will move in among them and softly talk to them? Even when danger is near, he doesn't necessarily point out the predator to the flock and cause panic. No, he moves to place himself in between the flock and the danger and does what is needed until the threat is passed."

As they walked a little farther, Narrac continued. "If you watch closely, you'll notice that people and sheep have a lot in common. If you tell people what they want to hear, be it truth or not, they will listen and pay attention. And those who are really good at it can even get people to do their bidding. Take the priests in the temple, some are good and kind, but many others just exploit the people to increase their wealth and public standing. Even our king manipulates the people by telling them what they want to hear while taking what he wants. Taxes are an example, one man's way to enslave another man."

Matthew interrupted. "I thought the Romans were the ones who collected taxes."

Narrac shook his head. "Yes, they do, but the king gets a part of the taxes collected by the Romans and from the temple. Someday, just someday, I hope I get to see the high and 'mighties' of this world brought down. Ah, but that's nothing more than a shepherd's dream." Narrac looked down at Matthew. "I was very impressed with the way you handled yourself earlier with the hawk. You keep that up and pay attention and you'll make a first-rate sheepherder."

Matthew walked a little straighter. "Do you think I could be as good as Malich?"

"All things are possible; all things are possible," Narrac mused.

The new location was a shallow valley with a small brook running through the middle. To say the grass was green and lush would be an over-statement, but compared to the last location, this was a sheep Eden. The brook ran to a small field of large rocks where it disappeared below one of the larger structures; past the other side of the valley lay a barren stretch southward. To the left, sprouting from the landscape was a small town. The clay brick buildings could be seen shimmering in the late day heat. Out of the barren southern expanse seemed to be a caravan of shapes trudging their way toward the gritty town.

Matthew decided that he was lucky to be in this place closer to water than out on that very dry trek. Matthew could see all of the sheep that had collected themselves at the brook. Malich came back up to the lip of the valley to join Matthew and Narrac.

"They'll be easy to watch from here for a little bit. As soon as they could smell the water, there was no holding them back. I was able to side step the onrush when we came over the lip of this valley," Malich said as he approached the two.

Matthew pointed to the south. "Is that a caravan from Egypt?"

Shading his eyes, Narrac said, "I don't think it's a merchant caravan, not enough camels. It looks like an exodus from some famine area."

"No," remarked Malich. "Last week, I met a traveler who brought word that everyone must return to their ancestries' hometown for a census, by Rome."

"Again with the Romans," spat Narrac. "Now they want to count us to see if they can squeeze any more out of us. Or maybe they just want to get us all into one place, so they can select new servants and send us back to Egypt!"

Malich stepped closer to Narrac. "Enough, Narrac." Malich halfway glanced toward Matthew who was standing there wide-eyed. Malich con-tinued, placing his hand on Matthew's shoulder. "None of that will happen. The Romans are just taking an accounting of their empire. Like any good merchant, one must take inventory every so often. It is nothing more."

"Well, they must be in dire need to be counting the table scraps in a place like this," Narrac replied.

Malich lifted his staff. "In the next couple of days, we shall go to the city of David and be added to the census. Other shepherds are coming to the area. My cousin Joshua will watch the flock while we are gone." Narrac raised both of his hands in surrender and walked off toward the flock.

Matthew stared up at Malich. "Are we in trouble? Are the Romans going to take us away?"

"No," comforted Malich. "Narrac is just upset. And when he gets upset, he says things that are wild and empty. Forget what you've heard; everything will be all right."

"But how do you know?" questioned Matthew.

"It's the belief of God's promise to Abraham. We shall be a mighty nation, which will number more than the grains of sand by the sea. What a waste it would be, the tighter the Romans and the king squeeze the people, the louder they will become. And the louder the people become, the more they squeeze."

"How will it end?" asked Matthew.

Malich hesitated. "The prophets say that a new king will come and lead the nation into a new world. Some think he will arise from a great house with power. Others think he will be like Gideon, a mighty warrior who will drive the Romans from our homes."

Matthew asked, "Who do you think it will be?"

"I don't know," responded Malich. "God never seems to do anything the same way twice, and it is usually not the way any of us expect. For myself, a simple shepherd, I think the flock is more than enough. Besides, people need to eat and need wool for blankets and clothing."

"It is time; I think the sheep have drunk well. It's time to put them up before night. Narrac, it's time," Malich called. "Matthew, work your way around on the right. Don't let any stray farther down the brook. We'll move the flock over to the grouping of rocks. There's an area where we can pen in the sheep, where they'll be safe. There's only one way in, and we'll block that with limbs to create a gate."

Matthew asked, "How do you know all of this?"

Malich replied as he moved toward the flock, "This is part of my ancestor's land. Now get moving, we need to be done before dark."

And with that, the three moved to their respective positions with Malich leading a somewhat more reluctant flock toward the rocky pen. With not too much urging, the flock moved to their evening resting place. And as fate would have it, the last wooly charge to enter the pen was the mischievous lamb. The lamb tried to dodge Narrac and almost ran over Matthew. But with a bleat from its mother, the lamb turned tail and bounced into the pen. As Malich stepped through the pen's opening, Narrac started placing branches across the opening.

"There's always one that wants to make things difficult. And it figures it would be your lamb," commented Narrac.

"Well, the task is done," remarked Malich. "Let's set up camp over there, where we can watch the opening to the pen. I think we have done well for today. And I seem to be a little hungry, is anyone else?"

Matthew's ear to ear grin spoke volumes and not a single word was needed.

"A small fire would be nice," added Narrac. "Matthew, let's collect some wood and brush. A little extra warmth will help stay the cold night."

"And any predators," added Malich. Placing their bundles down, which they had carried to the new campsite, Narrac and Matthew started collecting fuel while Malich went to the brook to fill their waterskins.

# CHAPTER 8

Night fell as a velvet blanket. And the stars glittered in the night sky. Even though the day had been hot, night was becoming cold. A small fire lay in the middle, illuminating the faces of its onlookers. And in the dark, only stillness looked upon the three with interest and wonder.

Matthew asked, "What happened to my mother and father?" Malich and Narrac looked at each other.

Narrac was the first to respond. "Don't you remember? We've discussed this before." Malich motioned with his hand for Narrac to settle down.

"Matthew, you've seemed a little confused and distracted lately. Are you feeling well?"

Matthew looked from one to the other and then back into the fire.

"Yes, I'm fine. I just want to hear you tell me again," Matthew replied. Malich's gaze left Matthew and fell into the fire.

"Well," Malich began, "your father was with a group of zealots who believed that if they would fight the Romans, the Messiah would come to their aid and destroy the Roman army. He was captured after he was wounded, when the raiding party he was with attacked a Roman supply caravan. God was merciful; your father died of his wounds before he could be tortured and then executed. Your mother was sick with an illness carried in by a caravan from the East. She was too weak with the fever and died. That's when my wife, your mother's sister, brought you to our home."

Narrac added, "This is home now, we're family now." Matthew looked over at Narrac and then Malich. He nodded and gave a halfhearted smile.

"It's all right, I just wanted to hear again. When do you want me to take the watch over the flock?"

Malich looked over at Narrac and said, "I'll take the first watch. You two get some rest, and I'll wake Narrac to take my place. You can wake Matthew before sunrise to take the final watch of the night."

Narrac lay back on a boulder, reclined with his head resting on part of the bundle he was carrying earlier in the day. Matthew lay down, still gazing into the fire and pulling his coat up about him. Malich found a perch on another rock where he was able to keep one ear on the flock and still watch over the two companions preparing for sleep. Except for a minor pop or whispered hiss from the fire, it was a quiet night, a silent night.

Light, a brilliant light shown all around; but it was not blinding. The fire, which had been the only source of illumination within the encampment, seemed to have lost all heat and glow. Matthew pushed himself up and noticed that there was no shadow under him where he was laying. Everything seemed to be illuminated, including his own clothing.

"Do not be afraid." Matthew looked up and standing on the other side of the fire, between Narrac and Malich, stood a man with his head hooded and his palms held out, down by his sides. He was glowing, or his cloths, or both. Matthew, Narrac, and Malich stared frozen at the figure. The hands rose up and pulled back the hood to reveal the most beautiful and perfect face they had ever seen. There was warmth and caring in the face that appeared to glow with the same radiance as the hood that was removed.

The stranger continued, "I bring you tiding of great joy and for all people. For on this day, in the city of David, a savior is born, Christ the Lord. And this shall be a sign to you. You shall find the baby wrapped in swaddling clothes and lying in a manger." His voice was like music, soft, and reassuring. As he lifted his hands up over his head, he gazed up.

And there were angels, hundreds, thousands, more than Matthew could count or even imagine. Some were circling, some were moving down toward the camp, while others were moving away from them. And there were more; so many more, just there, everywhere. They were so beautiful. Each had a glow of a faint color that pulsed with the different rhythms of the music. The music was not just in the air, but it was inside the body, flowing to and fro.

The angels were singing praises to God. "Glory, glory, glory to God in the highest, and on Earth peace, good will toward men," the singing continued.

Matthew had never heard or felt anything like this before. Any fear he had was washed away during these brief moments. Then the stranger among the three was drawn up, along with the light and music, into one bright point in the night sky. The new star extended a faint shaft of light down to a spot near the far side of the town.

"Hey, what's happening?" All three jumped. It was Joshua clambering up the slope to their camp. "We saw a light, so bright. What was going on? What were you doing?"

Malich, Narrac, and Matthew just looked at each other. Malich turned to face Joshua. "Can you stay and watch the sheep?"

Joshua responded, "What is going on?"

"Can you stay and watch the flock? We'll be back before sunrise," Malich repeated.

"Well yes, I can stay," said Joshua.

"Good, we'll explain everything when we get back," Malich said as he motioned to the other two to follow along. Narrac picked up his coat that had slid off and wrestled it back on. Matthew grabbed his crook and followed after Malich and Narrac.

Narrac questioned Malich, "What do you plan to say about what just happened? How are we going to explain . . ."

Malich kept on walking. "I don't know, but we'll have plenty of time to figure it out." And the three walked on toward the little town of Bethlehem.

# CHAPTER 9

Bethlehem, a small, dusty town in the corner of seemingly nowhere, was quiet for its swelling population. By this time of night, the Roman guard had retired to their encampment on the far side of town. Lights shown in many of the windows, and sounds of revelry emanated from some of the doorways. But the shepherds' gazes were fixed on the single shaft of faint light which was falling on a thatched awning attached to the side of a hill, next to one of the town's dwellings. The closer they approached to the thatched awning, the stiller the night became, and the dimmer the sounds of Bethlehem became.

Above the half door, lamplight could be seen. Malich peered into the stable and gently pushed the door open. As Malich, Narrac, and Matthew entered, the shaft of starlight pierced the thatched awning and fell upon a sleeping baby, wrapped in swaddling clothes and lying in a straw-filled manger just as the stranger had described.

Matthew was the first to approach the feeding trough. And as he did, he dropped to his knees while leaning on his crook. Narrac and Malich flanked Matthew and leaned over, resting on their staffs. The babe was common looking, nothing special could be seen. This did not look like a king or a warrior, just a sleeping baby. And yet, there was a feeling of calm, peace, safety—love. Here lay the praises of heaven, in a common stable.

Malich looked up and for the first time realized that they were not alone. Back off to one side were a man and woman. The woman was half reclining on a pile of straw against the wall, and the man was crouching beside her. The woman looked tired to Malich, but she had the glow of being a new mother. The man started to rise, but the woman laid her hand on his forearm, staying his motion. At this, Narrac also noticed the pair and looked over at Malich. Malich motioned with his head, and they moved over to the couple.

"Please, excuse our intrusion," offered Malich.

Narrac jumped in. "We had to come and see, after—"

Malich started, "Please, my name is Malich, and this is Narrac. Our young friend is Matthew. We were in the fields outside of town, watching over our sheep when . . ."

The man said, "Please, continue."

So Malich continued, explaining about the stranger.

"The angel," Narrac corrected.

Malich continued with the description of the light, the music, and the angels. And when they told the man and woman the angel's message, the woman squeezed the man's arm.

"I know this sounds impossible and unbelievable, but how else would we know to come here now?" ended Malich. "But you must be tired and need your rest." Malich looked down at the woman. "We will leave now. Thank you, for you two are the most blessed, having God's favor." He motioned toward the manger. Malich and Narrac bowed to the man and woman and turned to return to their original positions by Matthew.

During the entire conversation, Matthew did not move. He just knelt there staring at the baby. Only once did he look away due to a familiar sound, a crying lamb. It was over to one side of the stable, lying next to its mother. The ewe nosed the lamb, and it quieted down. For a brief moment, Matthew could have sworn that it was his lamb, but then, he realized this lamb had different markings. And with that, Matthew's gaze was back on the baby. And when he looked back into the manger, the baby was awake and staring back at Matthew. The eyes looked caring and happy. Matthew thought for a moment the baby was even smiling at him. It did not matter, because Matthew was smiling enough for both of them. It seemed as though the babe was trying to tell Matthew something; something that he should already know. But Matthew was unable to understand or think of what it might be. The one thing he did know was that there was warmth in that gaze that he felt he had never seen before nor would ever see again.

The next thing Matthew realized was that Malich and Narrac were lifting him back to his feet saying, "It's time Matthew; we need to go back to the flock." As they walked back through the stable door, Malich pulled the half door closed and stole one more glance at the scene of the new family.

As they started walking through the town, back the way they had come, Malich spoke, "And this is the beginning."

"Beginning to what?" Narrac questioned.

"I'm not sure," responded Malich. "But this is not the end; it is definitely the start of something great. Remember the angel said a savior is born, Christ the Lord."

Right then, the three were passing by an inn and out stumbled five of its patrons. For a still night, the five were like a midsummer's thunderstorm, yelling, singing, and shouting. Matthew pressed in close to Malich as they approached the ruckus bunch.

Narrac was the first to address one of the noisy rabbles. "Quiet down! Is there no decency among you? There is a family with a newborn, right over there."

"What, in that stable? You shepherds treat the sheep like family, like children. I think they're best on a spit and roasted. I don't need to be quiet for livestock," roared one of the drunks.

Narrac responded, "You don't understand; you don't understand. I'm not talking about sheep. There's a woman who has just given birth to a baby, a . . . savior." With that the bunch quieted down.

Another of the drunks responded, "What? A savior? Whose savior? What are you saying?"

Malich moved in. "Be still and listen." Matthew recognized the tone of voice that Malich was using, the same as when he talked to the sheep. Malich continued, "Over in that stable is a child, a baby, who is different, special. See that star?" Malich pointed up. "See how the light shines down and falls on the roof of the stable? Do you see it falling anywhere else? No? Just on that stable."

Narrac jumped in. "It's a light from heaven, a window—"

Malich raised a hand. "We were in the fields watching over the sheep when a man, an angel, appeared before us. He told us about the baby being born and how we would find it wrapped in swaddling clothes and laying in a manger. Who would lay their child in an animal's feeding trough?"

One of the more sober revelers asked, "What else were you told?"

By this time, a small crowd had started to gather, listening to the exchange. Malich and Narrac looked at each other, but it was Matthew that spoke up. "He said that the baby was our savior, Christ the Lord."

Another of the revelers who was not as sober said, "Are you going to listen to this; it's crazy talk from a bunch of sheepherders." And with that, he staggered off through the crowd in the opposite direction.

The first reveler waved the second off and continued, "Was there anything else said?"

Matthew again jumped in. "There were angels everywhere; and they were singing, 'Glory to God in the highest.'"

Narrac and Malich joined in. "And on Earth peace and good-will to all men."

The reveler said, talking to the crowd, "Doesn't Micah say in the Scriptures that 'Bethlehem though you are little among the thousands of Judea, yet out of you shall he come forth unto me that is to be ruler of Israel'? And remember the words of Isaiah, 'For unto to us a child is born, unto us a son is given; and the government shall be upon his shoulders, and his name shall be called Wonderful, Counselor, the Mighty God, the everlasting Father, the Prince of Peace.'"

All stood in silence while their gaze shifted from the shepherds, to the star, and back down to the stable's thatched awning and lamplit door. Then by ones and twos, the crowd with a couple of the revelers drifted toward the stable. They gathered around the doorway, peering at the sight within.

Malich turned to Narrac and Matthew. "We need to get back. Joshua will think we have run off." And with that, the three melted into the darkness as they left the sleepy town behind.

As they approached their camp, they saw Joshua tending their small fire while constantly looking up at the night sky. "Joshua," Malich called out. "We're back."

"Where did you go? What's been going on? What was that bright light? From over where I was resting it looked like daytime here earlier. That's why I came to see."

Malich responded, "Joshua have a seat, and I will try to answer your questions." As they were taking their places around the fire, Malich looked over at Matthew. "Would you go and check on the flock? I've not heard a sound out of them, and there should have been some stirring as we approached." Matthew nodded and walked out of the firelight over to the makeshift pen.

As Matthew's eyes adjusted to the starlight, he could see the wooly clumps, quietly lying in the pen. Quietly, Matthew counted as best he could in the starlight to see if all were there. Near the end of his count, he noticed his lamb lying next to his mother.

A quiet voice in his head said, "Peace on Earth and good will to all men." He said to himself, "I guess that included the sheep, too. Even you, little one," looking at the lamb. Matthew then headed back to the firelit circle and Malich's and Narrac's explanations to Joshua.

As he was sitting down, Malich was telling Joshua about following the shaft of starlight to the stable in town. Matthew lay down and covered himself with his coat. As he lay there listening to the story of that night, Matthew felt sleep wrap around him and gently drag him into the darkness of slumber.

# CHAPTER 10

Before his eyes were open, Matthew heard the crying of the lamb. He was so tired from being up most of the night; he just wanted to get more sleep. But the lamb was in trouble or getting into trouble. Matthew opened his eyes and started to stand up and then froze. His rocky, desert-like surroundings were gone. He was sitting in a boulder field once again. And his hands, they were no longer small and brown but large, fair, and strong. And he was wrapped in his traveling cloak.

It must have been a dream, but it was so real. And then there was the crying of the lamb. He grabbed a hold of this walking staff and stood up. Matthew then realized that it was getting dark and had become colder. Clouds had moved in, so it was difficult to gauge how late it really was. Matthew knew that he had slept way too long and needed to find the town before night fell. If not, he would be spending a very cold night in a place he did not know and was not prepared for. But there was that sound of a lamb crying. He needed to investigate that first and then hurry on down the path while he could still make out the path. With his mind still reeling, he started his search for the troubling sound.

After weaving around a number of boulders, he found the source of the sound, a small bundle wedged down between a couple of boulders. As Matthew reached down, he said, "It's all right, don't be afraid."

Right then a tearful face looked up at him. It was familiar; and yet, he was unsure. Then it hit him, this was the small child that had run into him at the train station upon his arrival.

The child, with a small shivering voice said, "Cold."

Matthew swept up the child and wrapped the little icicle next to him under his cloak. Matthew felt the heat of his body being sucked away, and after a few minutes, the child ceased shivering and shifted to be more comfortable.

Matthew looked down. "What's your name, little one?"

The child looked up. "Rachel. Are you going to tell Father Gates I was out here? I'm not supposed to go to the train station by myself. But I wanted to see if my mommy had come home to get me."

Matthew was starting to strain his eyes to discern the path.

Matthew responded, "I was the only one that got off the train today. Do you know when your mother is returning?"

Rachel said, "No, I was hoping today."

Matthew asked, "Rachel, how old are you?"

"I'm five, and I'll be six tomorrow. Are you going to tell Father Gates that I was at the station?" Rachel asked again.

With a little concern in his voice, Matthew said, "I hope we'll be able to find Father Gates. Do you know where the town is?"

Rachel wriggled an arm free of Matthew's cloak and pointed, "Right down there," and quickly pulled her hand back into her warm cocoon.

Right then, Matthew rounded a small outcropping where the trees parted and there nestled in a shallow valley lay Bethell. The town was larger than Matthew had expected. In the dusk, he could see soft lights starting to illuminate the windows of the modest dwellings. The path down to the town was visible but starting to fade with the light. And then a snow flake tapped Matthew on the nose. He looked down at Rachel, finding her asleep in his arms, wrapped by the cloak.

Matthew smiled, thinking to himself, *Just like the little lamb in my dream.* And yet it seemed so real, the heat, the smells, and he could still remember the taste of the bread and cheese that he had had for dinner in the dream. He slipped on a stone in the path but caught himself with his walking stick. Quietly, "I guess I better keep my mind on getting down to town." He checked Rachel; she appeared to be still asleep.

The darker it got, the heavier the snow fell. Just as the sky gave up its light, Matthew entered the edge of Bethell. Everything looked so peaceful, just like one of those hand-painted Christmas cards. The snow was just thick enough to give a glow to the buildings and street. Now that he was here, he realized he was not sure where to go. He did not know where to find Father Gates. He was about to wake Rachel when he heard music; no, it was singing, beautiful singing.

Matthew started walking toward the singing. He was wondering how something so angelic sounding could be in a place like this. It was almost as beautiful as the singing in his dream. Still there was that nagging feeling about the dream, but it did not feel like a dream.

He was feeling more confused when a voice called out to him. "Matthew? Father Matthew, is that you?" From the shadow of a doorway, of what looked like a large barn, a figure appeared. It was limping and after a step or two leaned against some sort of staff.

Matthew called out, "Malich?"

The figure shifted. "It's Father Gates. We were just preparing to send out search parties to find you and one other."

Matthew walked over to Father Gates. As he approached Gates, he could see a man dressed in a similar cloak but much more worn. He had a cheerful face, but it had seen a number of years and a lot of miles.

Matthew said, "Father Gates, it is so good to meet you. You said you were getting ready to look for me and someone else?"

"Yes," replied Gates. "One of our orphans disappeared this afternoon. She has a habit wondering off, looking for her mother."

Matthew stepped a little closer and pulled back the corner of his cloak. "Would this be your little lost lamb?" offered Matthew.

With glee Gates responded, "Rachel . . . Praise the Lord! How did you find her? Where did you find her?"

Matthew said, "I came across her on the path from the train station. She was cold and worn out. As soon as she got warm, she fell asleep. What was she doing at the train station?"

Gates shook his head. "Rachel is looking for her mother. She must have heard several of us talking about you arriving on the train and thought her mother was on the train. You see, tomorrow is her birthday, and she thinks that her mother will be here for her birthday."

Matthew questioned, "When is her mother supposed to return?"

Gates made a grimace. "I don't think she will ever return. You see, Rachel's father was killed in a mining accident, and her mother went mad and abandoned Rachel when she was four. The mother left a note apologizing, saying that she was not fit to take care of Rachel and that she was leaving."

Matthew looked down at Rachel. "So, Rachel doesn't know that her mother is not returning?"

"No," replied Father Gates. "But," continued Gates, "you're both here and just in time for the Christmas Eve service." With that Rachel stirred and, looking around, saw Father Gates.

She looked down into the cloak. "I know I wasn't supposed to go to the station by myself, but I wanted to see mommy," offered Rachel.

Father Gates stated with a frown that melted into a form of resignation. "It's okay now. Thankfully, Father Matthew here found you and brought you home. If he had not found you, I would hate to think what might have happened to you."

Rachel replied, "I know. I won't do it again. I just thought mommy would be here for my birthday."

"I understand," Father Gates reassured. "Are you hungry?"

"Yes," responded Rachel.

"Well, head on over and find Mrs. Baker. She'll get something for you shortly. Now off with you," directed Father Gates.

Rachel started to wriggle, and Matthew set her down. She took off across the street to a picturesque-looking cottage that had light streaming from three of its windows.

As Rachel reached the door, she knocked once and opened the door. As light beamed through the doorway, Matthew could hear a woman exclaimed, "Rachel, where have you been? I've been worried sick." Just then a head popped out of the door and waved to the two men.

Father Gates waved back. "Please see that she gets something to eat. I don't think she'll be wandering off any time soon." And with that the head popped back inside and the door closed.

# CHAPTER 11

Matthew was once again aware of the singing. "That music, it is so pure and clean," Matthew remarked.

Father Gates glanced over his shoulder at the building. "Yes, one of the many blessings with this region. You see the Welsh have perfect pitch and are known worldwide for their singing. Most of the people here are second and third generation Welsh miners. It makes one feel that you're just that much closer to heaven. Now, come along. We have a Christmas Eve service to perform. It won't be very elaborate or glorious. But it's the best that we can do under the circumstances."

Matthew started walking toward the building, and Father Gates turned limping beside him.

They entered a door into a dimly lit coatroom. Father Gates offered, "You can set your cloak and staff over here." To Matthew's surprise, there on the floor sat his books and things. Gates continued, "I asked Mr. Felder to leave your things here for now. Later, I'll get some help to move your things to the cottage that I use when I'm here."

"Thank you," replied Matthew.

Gates paused at the next set of doors with his hand on the latch. "Ready to meet the people of Bethell?"

Matthew responded, "Before we go in, I would like to confess something. I had my focus on a big cathedral in a major city. When I found out I was assigned to Bethell, I thought I was being punished for who I am. But now I've realized, it's not about me, it's about others. And right now, this is the most beautiful cathedral I have been privileged to enter. . . . Yes, I think I am now ready."

With a smile, Gates opened the door leading into the church. As he did so, the light and music from within flooded the coatroom. Those excellent Welsh singers had just started singing "Hark the Herald Angels Sing."

Both men were infused with the environment they were entering. Matthew entered first, followed by Father Gates. Gates drew the door closed, but the latch did not catch. The door quietly creaked open, casting a slender column of light into the cloak room.

The illumination fell on Matthew's belongings, one item in particular, his walking staff. There, in the light, the shepherd's crook rested against the wall. It was a crudely hewn wooden staff with a twisted hook. And if one looked close enough, they would find a series of scratches on the hook of the crook. For, would not one expect to find a good shepherd with his crook?

—Book 2—

# WITNESS COINS

# CHAPTER 1

There it hung, weathered and aged, but you could still read the name "Bethell" even with the slightly faded "t." The early spring mist drizzle created little droplets along the bottom edge of the sign. Every so often a drop would free itself and fall to the puddle near the edge of the railway platform where Matthew Brooks, or now Father Matthew, was standing. He was staring into the receding image of the train as it faded into the misty fog. His thoughts and feelings were mixed with the departure of Father Griffith.

Even though they had only met a little over a year ago, Matthew had learned so much from Father Griffith. They had traveled to numerous camps and villages in the area to provide aid and support where possible, but they always ended back at Bethell. During the trips Father Griffith explained the history of the area, which mainly focused on coal mining. A few of the villages existed for other reasons, but one way or the other, they tied back to coal. Every so often Father Griffith would ask Matthew about his "experience" the day he arrived in Bethell and the shepherd's staff Matthew always carried. Many an hour was spent trying to determine the significance of the experience, for both agreed that there was something more than just a dream.

But what and why, to Matthew, was a mystery. Matthew had shared, somewhat sheepishly, his initial thoughts and feelings with Father Griffith when he first learned of his assignment to Bethell. Matthew remembered the hardy laugh that Father Griffith gave with this sharing. He remembered Father Griffith explaining a somewhat similar feeling when he first arrived at Bethell.

One thing Father Griffith said would always stick with Matthew. "We are but hirelings to watch over our Master's flock, no matter to what valley or mountaintop they may have wandered."

When the letter came last month informing Father Griffith that he was to be transferred to a new position, Matthew knew this time would come. This was the whole reason he had been sent to Bethell. But he felt there was so much more he could learn from Father Griffith. Matthew was not prepared to be on his own. He knew how to perform the different services depending on the nature of the time and need. The funeral and wake ceremonies were ones he least liked to perform. Even though he had been taught the standard sayings, nothing seems to ease the loss of a loved one, especially one who died at an early age. Only time seemed to take the edge off of the loss.

The other thing that bothered Matthew was that there seemed to be many more funerals than other, more joyous ceremonies like baptisms, christenings, and marriages. Now with Father Griffith leaving, he felt like he was presiding over another funeral. Next week he would start traveling around to the other villages in his parish. . . . His parish, not Father Griffith's parish . . . but his. It just finally hit him that it was now *all* his responsibility.

There was one other strange thing that tickled at the back of Matthew's mind: why did a bishop come to collect Father Griffith? Bishop Mayweather seemed to be an amiable person. Even though Father Griffith had explained that the two of them had attended school together, it still seemed odd that a bishop would travel all the way to Bethell and in such dismal weather.

The three days they had spent together prior to their departure seemed relaxed and sociable, but on two occasions Mayweather had asked about Matthew's shepherd's staff and Mathew's "experience." Father Griffith told Matthew it was alright to share the "experience." Even though little was said by Mayweather, Matthew felt that his words were being weighed and analyzed. After the second time the bishop seemed to be a little nervous and did not ask anything further concerning the "experience."

The remainder of their time together was in discussing the different residents of the parish; the local orphanage, which Father Griffith had started; and the general goings-on in a coal mine town.

Now the ghostly image of the last car of the train melted into the fog. As Matthew started to turn, he looked up at the depot sign to see a drop or two separate and join the rest of their droplets on the depot platform. Matthew turned and shook his travel cloak as if to shake off the thoughts of the past few minutes.

At the other end of the platform was the station master, Mr. Haddor, leaning out of the depot door. "You two," he hollered and waiving a hand at two men moving boxes and barrels. "Is everything loaded in the wagon?"

One of the workers raised a hand with a thumbs-up.

"Good. . . . Well, come out of the weather and warm yourselves. I can't heat the platform from one little coal stove." The two men hurried over to the door and entered as Mr. Haddor stepped back inside to let them pass. Haddor was just starting to shut the door when he noticed Matthew walking up the platform. "Father Matthew, I didn't see you; would you like to come in and warm up before riding back to town?"

Father Matthew paused by the door and saw that the two men had shed their hats and coats and were warming themselves by the stove. Matthew inquired, "Is Pappy in there?"

Haddor glanced over his shoulder and responded, "No, he was supervising these two in the loading of the wagon. I think he's still with the wagon. Won't you come in?"

Matthew glanced around the corner of the depot to where the wagon stood. "Thank you, I'm going to check on Pappy. If he's going straight to town, I'll ride with him. If I can convince him to come warm up first . . . we'll be back in a minute."

Haddor retorted, "Knowing him he'll be heading back. I've never heard nor seen him being affected by the weather. I don't know how he does it. This damp rain works on my joints something fierce. Father, could you say a prayer for my joints, short one if you'd please? I'd like to get back to the coal stove."

Matthew smiled, slightly tipped his head, and started "Dear merciful Father, please give some relief to Mr. Haddor's joints during the wet spring weather. Amen."

Haddor echoed, "Amen. . . . Thank you, Father. I need to go back and tend the stove. If you convince Pappy to warm up just come on in." With that the door closed but only after a little nudging from the inside, seeing how the door's wooden frame had swelled in the rain.

Matthew turned, still smiling and headed around the corner of the depot to the loaded wagon.

# CHAPTER 2

One could just barely make out the "Bethell 17" on the side of the green faded wagon. Various boxes and barrels had been hastily stacked on to the bed of the wagon. Coils of rope and cable hung from the sides of the wagon. Pappy, John Felder, was adjusting harness on one of two mules hooked to the wagon.

Pappy looked up as Matthew approached. "Father Matthew, are you ready to head back to town?"

"Mr. Haddor was wondering if you'd be interested in coming into the station and warming up before heading back. I, myself, am ready to go whenever you are ready," responded Matthew.

"There's no need warming up just to get cold again on the trip back. Besides, Arthur and Gwen would prefer getting back and into a nice dry barn before evening," he said, motioning to the two mules. "Time's a-wasting Father, let's get started," Pappy stated as he started climbing up onto the wagon.

Matthew watched the small but very spry gentleman clamber up on the wagon. Matthew would have guessed that Pappy was in his late fifties and was surprised to learn from Father Griffith that Pappy was seventy-two, soon to be seventy-three in another month. As Pappy settled onto the wagon seat and started to reach for the reins, he motioned to Matthew to climb up next to him. First Matthew passed up his shepherd's staff to Pappy, who cocked it at an angle next to him on the seat. Matthew climbed up but found that parts of the wagon foot holds were very slippery, making his ascent a little slower than that of Pappy.

Finally, Matthew settled next to Pappy. Pappy reached over, released the wagon's hand brake, gave a quick flick with the reins, and Arthur and Gwen started off on the stone packed road to Bethell. As Pappy had mentioned, the mules seem to know the sooner they were back, the sooner they would be out of the weather. The wagon rolled along at a fairly good clip. Not much was said at first on the ride back. But eventually there was a rather sharp lurch to the left and then back level as one of the wagon's wheels found an unseen and sizable pothole.

"Easy there Arthur, Gwen. We don't need to lose a wheel in this weather. Sorry about that, Father, it is a little difficult to see where the holes are with all of the water on the road," said Pappy.

"Not a problem, Mr. Felder" responded Matthew.

Pappy cocked an eye at Matthew, "Now Father, I would prefer if you called me Pappy like everyone else. I've done my time down below and outlasted most of my peers so Pappy seems a more fitting name for myself. Besides Mr. Felder sounds a little too respectable for someone like myself. If you had known me back in my youth you would probably have a few other names you would prefer to call me and rightly so. I was uh . . . high spirited in my early days."

Matthew, with a smirkish grin, "Alright Mr. Fel—" Matthew caught himself, "Pappy. Provided you call me just Matthew. The title of Father is not something I've quite gotten used to, especially now with Father Griffith gone."

"Miss him, do you," replied Pappy.

"Yes. I feel as though there was so much more I needed to learn from Father Griffith. He has such insight into the happenings of everyone around here. He knew what to say and how to say it. Especially in the most difficult times," mused Matthew. "I just wished I had more time with Father Griffith before Mayweather came to collect him."

"That Mayweather fella, you said he's a bishop?" asked Pappy.

"Yes," replied Matthew.

Pappy continued, "I always wondered what a bishop was. I've been playing chess for years with Jim, Todd, Frank, and a few others, but I never understood what a bishop did. I mean a knight or a rook, castle, seem to make sense. A castle moves side to side or forwards and backwards, like a wall. A knight moves in an "L" shaped path, like someone riding a horse around an obstacle to attack his opponent. But the bishop, moving diagonally, always seemed a little strange. But after meeting that Mayweather fella and seeing how he talked, he never did answer a question directly. Always seemed to sort of give an answer but not necessarily to the question that was asked. I guess that's what bishops come at you diagonally on the board, never head on."

Matthew stared off down the road, mulling over what Pappy had just said. After a few moments Matthew reflected, "That does make a lot of sense. I just realized that on two occasions I asked Bishop Mayweather why he had come to get Father Griffith. He would always respond with 'I needed to get out of the office' or 'It was good to see what my old friend had been up to these many years.'"

Pappy chuckled, "Our living conditions, way of life didn't seem to be too much to his liking. The first time he met several of the men coming off shift from the hole he recoiled, like they had the plague. The way he moved to put you and Father Griffith between himself and the lads. I don't think he is the outdoors type. And this morning he seemed a little annoyed to ride in the wagon with you and Father Griffith to the depot."

"I noticed the same thing," Matthew added. "He did seem to have gotten up on the wrong side of bed this morning. And he was most anxious to get on the train once it had arrived. Like getting on would make the train leave sooner. Yes, I must agree he's more of a city mouse than a country mouse, as Father Griffith would say."

About that moment Pappy started pulling back on the reins, "Slow up there you two. We need to take this part a little slower." Pappy kept his eyes fixed on the road but said to Matthew, "There's a bit of a down grade coming up and the wet road makes things a little slick. I don't want to lose control of this fully loaded wagon. These two," referring to the mules, "know better. They done this hundreds of times. They're just wanting to get back to the barn and a bag of oats."

Changing the subject, Matthew asked, "Pappy, you said you used to work in the mine?"

Pappy nodded, "Seems like a lifetime ago but it's only been twelve years since I was last down in the hole." Pappy shivered, "Ever since then I've been hauling supplies for the mining company with Arthur and Gwen here."

Matthew noticed how Pappy said the "hole." He asked, "Pappy did something happen?"

Pappy sat there with a distant stare.

Matthew realized this may not be such a good question to have asked and added, "I'm sorry, I didn't mean to pry into something personal."

Pappy started, "It's alright son . . . I mean Father . . . Matthew." Pappy started shaking his head. "No, Father Griffith told me it was best to discuss the accident, not to bottle things up inside. . . . Down in the hole there is no night or day; no weather as we know on the surface. It's always now. The team I was on had just opened a new vein of coal. Since I was the smallest, I was able to wedge myself into tight areas to place the charges to widen the access to the vein. There were three others with me . . . Bob Thomas, Lenny Jones, and George Evans. You've met George's boys Seth and Samuel, the twins working in the hole. Anyway, I was placing the last of the charges when I heard the cracking and popping of stone. George, Bob, and Lenny yelled at me to get out and head for the main shaft. But in the blink of an eye the ceiling collapsed. They were alive one second and dead the next. I thought I was a goner. Entombed in the very rock that had given me a living for so many years. I was unharmed, but I was in a space that was no bigger than a broom closet. And I didn't know how long my air would hold out."

Pappy seemed distant so Matthew reached over to Pappy's arm, "It's ok; you don't need to continue."

Pappy reached over and patted Matthew's arm, "I'm ok. . . . I'm here, aren't I?" Pappy continued, "Once the dust had cleared, I relit my helmet lamp. My hands were shaking so bad I almost didn't get it lit." Matthew looked quizzically at Pappy, and Pappy noticed his expression. "You're wondering what I was doing with an old carbide lamp. Well, it was my dad's, and it never had let him down all the long years he had worked the coal veins. And I never did trust those new-fangled battery powered lamps. You see, you could shake the lamp and tell if there's water inside, and I always carried a few small lumps of calcium carbide in an oil cloth in my pocket. That way I always knew I had light. You can't shake one of those batteries and tell if you had twelve hours or twelve minutes of light. Anyway, I got the lamp lit and started to inspect the space around me. Most of it was solid slabs of stone and coal. I did locate a small pocket near where the ceiling had been, but there was no telling how far it ran, a few inches or a mile. Concerned about my air I put out the lamp. I lay there for hours, but it seemed like days. One's mind starts playing tricks. You start hearing things and even seeing things even though it's pitch black. Several times I thought I heard tapping on the rock and even voices. I thought I was going mad. But then I did hear something, a scraping and hammering. Even though I saw the ceiling collapse on them, I started calling out to Bob, Lenny, and George, thinking by some miracle they were safe and trying to dig me out. But when they got to me, it was young Jack Williams. You know the shift manager at the mine."

Matthew nodded, "He's come a long way in twelve years. All of the men I've talked to speak very highly of Jack."

"As they should," Pappy proudly offered. "Jack has stood up for the men regardless of what the mine owners wanted to do. If Jack didn't feel something was safe, he would push back on the mine owners. A time or two, I was surprised to see the owners back down and give in to Jack. Especially if he was able to show them how a few pieces of safety equipment or them hiring that geologist to periodically inspect the mine, and any new veins, would benefit them. Jack pointed out that a few dollars kept the mine from being shut down, stopping the flow of coal. The owner's black wealth. Stop the flow of coal and the owners have the same worth as any man jack in the mine . . . and maybe less." Pappy said something under his breath but Matthew couldn't make out what Pappy said.

Pappy then continued, "When I realized it wasn't one of the fellows trying dig me out, I went numb. I started to try and dig toward my rescuers, but it was of little use. I didn't have the room to swing a pick, even if I had one with me. But all I had was a busted drill shank I was using to shove the charges into the bore holes in the wall. Eventually, I saw a little light through that pocket I found earlier. Then I could hear Jack's voice calling to see who was at the other end of that pocket. To hear another voice when you think all is lost, there's nothing that can describe it. I'm not ashamed to admit, I bawled like a baby. Several hours later, Jack's hand came through the pocket. I grabbed his hand. I knew then that I was going to make it. As they widened the pocket, I was able to see several men moving rock and coal while others were shoring up the new ceiling. I was finally able to worm my way through the opening and into the tunnel with the others. Jack asked if anyone else was with me. I told him that Lenny, George, and Bob were standing right here when . . . That's when it struck me, to rescue me they had to dig through what was left of my three friends. I think Jack knew what I was thinking. He said it's ok, we have them. They'll be given to their families. I don't remember much after that until we left the mine. Just outside the entrance there were four coffins. Three were nailed shut and the fourth, the top set cross ways on the coffin, my coffin. At that moment I knew I would never go back into the hole." Pappy sat quiet and then said, "It was Jack who worked out the arrangement with the mine owners to give me the job of moving freight for the town. I've been doing this ever since. . . . I'm grateful to Jack. If it weren't for Jack, I'm not sure what I would have done."

Neither man spoke for some length of time. Matthew tried to imagine what it would have been like trapped in a small spot not knowing what would happen next. Matthew had been down in the mine a few times but more in the capacity of a tourist. Jack and two others had gone in for routine inspections and allowed Matthew to go along. Matthew had watched and asked questions about the mining operations and inspection points. He had been so busy taking in all of the information, as it was being explained to him, that he had never really thought about a cave-in. Besides, Jack and the others seemed so casual about the goings on that they might as well have been walking through the hillsides talking about the trees and local wildlife. But try as he might he could not quite place himself into Pappy's shoes.

As they got closer to town the weather had started to improve a little. The drizzle had stopped and things seemed to be a little brighter, not so dreary. Pappy had let the two mules pick up the pace a little and they appeared to be making pretty good time. Matthew asked, "You think we'll make it to town before dusk?"

Pappy responded, "Oh, at the rate Arthur and Gwen are going I think we should be there in an hour, well before dusk." Pappy took a side glance at Matthew and noticed that Matthew was half cradling and half leaning on his staff. Pappy inquired, "I've heard the story about you and that staff. I was wondering, was it a dream or were you really there?"

Now it was Matthew's turn to stare off into the distance. "I've asked myself the same thing many times, but I always come back to the same thing, the scratches that were on my hands and lower arms, and this staff. Of course, the scratches healed but there has always been the staff." Matthew looked at the staff in a questioning way and then back off into space. "Everything seemed so real. The images, the sounds and smells, even the language that I've never heard before, and yet, I still understood everything that was said. I can even remember the warmth of the small camp fire. Father Griffith and I have discussed this a number of times, but it remains a mystery. And the one part I will never forget was the way the baby looked at me. Such a knowing and caring expression. . . . I looked away but for a moment, and when I looked back the child was fast asleep, oblivious to his surroundings. I've never before or since had anything like that experience."

Pappy nodded, "I suspect that's why that Mayfield fella came here. Well around this next bend we'll be coming up on the final downgrade into the valley. Arthur and Gwen are starting to get anxious again. . . . Ease up there, you'll be home soon."

Even on such a dreary spring day the town seemed to be a picturesque setting with all of the several dozen houses, three shops, the church, and at the far end the mine entrance. Further around the side of the hill that filled one end of the valley one could just make out the rail system where coal emerged from the mine and into waiting coal carriers. Twice a week the heavy locomotives would come from the other side of the hill, delivering empty coal carriers on one track and leaving with the fully loaded coal carriers on the parallel loading track. There were two and sometimes three locomotives that would back the empty coal carriers onto the one side track, detach from the carriers, move back up the track about a tenth of a mile, and once the rail switch was moved back up onto the parallel side track to link with the full coal carriers. The whole operation took roughly an hour and totally fascinated Matthew. All his years growing up in the orphanage or when he was in school, he had never seen a train, except in a few photos or illustrations. None of those ever did any justice to these real metal giants.

But now the town seemed somewhat peaceful. There was smoke rising from several chimneys, probably in preparation for the evening meals.

# CHAPTER 3

Half way down the gentle sloping road into town, Gwen started shaking and acting like someone walking barefoot on hot coals. Pappy brought the two mules to a stop. "What is it, Gwen," Pappy questioned.

Suddenly both mules started shifting, shaking, and making a grunting noise.

"Oh no," Pappy all but whispered. "On with you," Pappy shouted as he snapped the reigns on the mules' backs.

Suddenly Matthew was grasping for any hand hold he could find. Both Arthur and Gwen were moving at a surprising gallop toward the town. Before Matthew could ask Pappy what had happened, he heard the siren at the mine start up. That could only mean one thing, there had been an accident in the mine.

Pappy shouted over the noise of the wagon flying down the road, "It's either a fire, cave-in, or a flooding. And by the way Gwen was acting, the odds are on a cave-in. Animals seem to be able to sense happenings in the Earth even though they may be several hundred feet down."

As they entered town, the buildings were a blur, but Matthew could still make out their residents emerging and running toward the mine entrance. Just when Matthew thought the mules, the wagon and its contents, and he and Pappy were going to smash into the weathered wooden building that was the mining office, Pappy pulled back on the reigns and put everything he had into the wagon's wheel brake. Matthew thought he heard Pappy say something about hold on, but he was doing a fair job of that already. The wagon and its contents, surprisingly, came to a stop with a couple of yards to spare. Matthew slipped a little in his seat but held his position. Pappy had wrapped the reins around the wagon brake lever and was down off of the wagon in what seemed one fluid motion.

By the time Matthew's feet were on the ground, Pappy was at the mining office door. But before Pappy could grab the door knob the door flew open, and there was Jack Williams. Jack and Pappy all but collided.

"Cave-in," Jack announced. The look on Pappy's face sent chills down Matthew's spine. Jack look at Pappy. "We got to go in and see what happened. We need four to go," continued Jack. "We need to stay in teams of two. There's a crew of six working the main vein in tunnel seven, and three others were doing tunnel inspections in one of three new sections, eleven, fourteen, and fifteen."

About that time, several of the town's residents started arriving, mainly women and children. Many of the miners had gone over to a union meeting at a mining camp in the next valley. It would be several hours before they were supposed to be returning. Normally there would have been roughly fifty workers in the mine. Those in the mine were making preparations so the miners returning from the union meeting would be able to pick up the next shift and maintain production goals.

Jack surveyed the crowd and pointed to two older men, Tom Thompson and Hal Martin. Matthew recognized both men who had recently retired from mining. Jack said, "I wouldn't ask, but every minute counts."

Tom looked at Hal and put his hand on his shoulder, "One more time?"

Hal nodded, "Aye, one more time for the lads."

Jack looked back through the crowd, but everyone else was either too old or too young. Jack's gaze fell back on Pappy.

"I can't Jack," said Pappy, "I just can't." Pappy hung his head.

Softly Jack said, "I understand, Pappy. I need you to start putting out calls for assistance and coordinate things while I'm below."

Pappy looked up with an almost astonished expression and said, "I can do that." Pappy then shifted past Jack and disappeared into the mining office.

Jack motioned, "Tom, Hal, let's get going." They started toward the access way to the mine.

Matthew spoke up, "Jack, you need one more, I can go."

Jack stopped in his tracks and wheeled around, "Father Brooks, I appreciate the offer, but I can't allow you in the mine." And with that Jack motioned to the other two, and they headed into the mine entrance cabin. Matthew followed the three into the equipment room.

"Jack, please hear me out," Matthew started.

Without missing a beat as Jack pulled on a set of coveralls, "Father, there's no way I can let you in the mine under these conditions. We don't know what we're facing. We don't know if there's a partial or total cave-in, flooding may have started. There's any number of things that may be happening. It too dangerous."

"Jack, I've been down three times, twice with you and once with Hal here," Matthew continued. "I've studied the mine's maps, and I know the procedures. Besides, you need a second. No one is to enter the mine by themselves. The buddy system is to be maintained at all times and in all situations."

Hal looked at Jack with a wry grin, "You know, he's right, Jack."

Jack stiffened, "Hal, you're not helping. Father Brooks, Matthew, I can't risk having anything happen to you down there. The mine owners would have my hide."

Matthew retorted, "What happens if something happens to you down there? How will anyone know where you've looked and not looked? And you've already pointed out that time is everything at this point."

Both Tom and Hal gave Jack that look that said *You know he's right*. Jack hesitated, "All right, but you're with me. And you will do exactly what I say without hesitation. Agreed?"

Matthew nodded.

"Alright," as Jack handed a pair of coveralls to Matthew, "Suit up, you're about Paul Simpson's size, these should fit."

As Matthew wriggled into the coveralls, Jack continued, "Tom, Hal, I need you two to go down to the main dig and see if you can find the work crew. The Father and I are going to look for the inspection crew. They should be in one of the new sections. If the main tunnel is blocked, go back to the elevator and report back to Pappy in the office. Use the phone at the base of the elevator shaft. If you get through to the crew and there's any issues with coming back to the main elevator shaft, see if everyone can get out at the coal lift. If you get out that way make sure to call Pappy from the train yard. Let him know the situation either way."

During this time Matthew found a pair of boots that seemed to fit.

"Tom, toss me Peterson's hat," Jack added. Jack handed the dingy yellow miner's helmet over to Matthew. "You may need to . . ." Jack's voice dropped off as he saw Matthew making the needed adjustments so that the helmet would properly fit his head.

Jack went to a cabinet and pulled out three battery packs and started handing them to the others. Instinctively, they clipped the packs to the coveralls belt and connected the helmet lamp cord to the packs. Jack reached back into the cabinet and retrieved a fourth pack and did the same. "These should give us twelve hours of light, but I want us all out within an hour, hour and a half max. Understood." Everyone nodded. "Alright let's go."

The four men left the equipment room, but before exiting, Jack, Hal, and Tom each picked up five-foot pry bars and handheld flashlights. Matthew followed still carrying his staff and a flashlight. Just before they reached the elevator car, all four stopped at the status board.

The status board was a gridwork of small pockets split into a right and left side. Above the left side there was one word, "UP," and on the right side another word, "DOWN." On the DOWN side there were two groups of cards, six in one cluster and three in another grouping.

Jack reached up and removed the six cards in the one grouping and started reading names. "You'll be looking for Al Banners, Fred Hughes, Don Jones, Kevin Spears, Ted Roberts, and John Lewis," talking to Tom and Hal. "And we'll be looking for," as Jack placed the six cards back on the board and picked up the other three, "Ben Davies, . . ." Jack hesitated, "the Evans twins, Samuel and Seth."

Tom shook his head while looking at the floor, "It will kill Evelyn if she loses the twins after losing George. I thought those two weren't supposed to be down in the mine at the same time."

Hal jumped in, "You know those two. They are both as stubborn as George was. Besides, have you ever seen one without the other? And if you did, it was next to impossible to tell which was which. Why I remember that time that they . . ."

Jack cleared his throat, "Hopefully we'll have time later to reminisce, but we need to be getting below. By chance, do you still have your cards?"

Tom already had his out and handed it to Jack as Hal reached into a pocket in the coveralls. Sheepishly Tom remarked, "I guess, it's habit, but whenever I leave the house, I grab it."

"Same here," as Hal handed his to Jack.

Jack placed their cards under the grouping of six cards. Next, he reached into his coverall pocket, removed his card, and placed under the group of three. He turned and looked at Matthew, "Father, the best thing for you is to lean your staff on the board. Everyone knows your staff and will know you're down in the mine." Matthew positioned the shepherd's staff so it rested over the grouping of three and Jack's card. "Ok, everyone into the elevator," Jack motioned.

After they were all on the elevator, Tom pulled the safety gate across the lift entrance, and Hal pressed the button and shifted the lever, starting the descent into the mine. Swiftly the walls scrolled by the elevator car's openings. No one said a word, although Tom seemed to be whispering something.

Hal looked at him, "Miner's Prayer?"

Tom nodded, then said, "I'd feel better if the good Father would say a few words."

Jack added, "Please, but do be quick, we're almost to the bottom of the shaft."

The elevator car started to slow.

Matthew hesitated, "Most merciful Father, please watch over these men and the others in this mine. Bring them all out safely and to their beds in their homes tonight."

And with that, there was a slight but abrupt bounce as the car reached the bottom. Jack pulled the safety gate back and stepped onto the mine floor. Each man followed a few steps from the elevator car then stopped as Jack turned to face them.

"Ok, no heroics. Find out where there is a collapse, see if you can find the digging crew, and get yourselves out the best way you know. If you come back to the elevator, use the phone," Jack pointed to the small box on the wall next to the car, "and report in with Pappy. If you get out the other way, use the phone in the train yard. Go."

Without hesitation, Tom and Hal switched on their head lamps and started out down the main tunnel leading to the digging crew. Very quickly the darkness in the tunnel seemed to swallow the light the two carried when they turned a corner.

Jack switched on his lamps and indicated that Matthew do the same. "We're going to section fourteen and fifteen first. We'll check eleven on our way out, if we haven't found them by then."

"Why eleven last?" inquired Matthew as they walked along the tunnel.

"If I know Ben, he'll start from the furthest point and work his way back. Besides, there's not been much digging in number eleven for the last several months. Dan Weise, our geologist, feels that vein is pretty much played out. Ben was in the office the other day when Dan was turning in his report. Here we are, the spur to the newer sections," Jack shined his light into a new path. "Start watching for debris on the floor and listen for any sounds," Jack instructed.

Matthew asked, "You mean voices?"

Jack replied, "Voices, yes, but also any snapping, popping, creaking, grinding or anything." The two moved on with only the crunching sounds of their footsteps on the mine floor. "Smell that?" Jack said to Matthew. "That's fresh coal dust. It's a good indication that the earth has been disturbed in the last few hours. There's not supposed to be any digging in this section. That's why Ben and the twins where here doing an inspection to determine if it was safe to start digging next week."

About that time Jack stopped and shined his head lamp up on a marker on the wall. "SECTION 11" could be clearly read. Jack shined his hand and head lamps into the void in the wall. "Do you hear or smell anything?" Jack asked.

Matthew strained his hearing but nothing. "No, not a sound, but the air doesn't seem to have the same . . ." he was searching for the right words, "dusty? It's cooler and seems damp."

"Very good," Jack told his student. "This is a good sign nothing has been disturbed, and if they were down there, they would have been out and back at the car with the first sign of trouble. Let keep going." They passed on down the passage, dark in front and dark behind. Periodically Jack would motion to stop and listen. Not hearing anything, they moved on. As they passed the sign marked "SECTION 12–13," Jack halted and the two stood perfectly still. The dry odor of coal dust was becoming stronger. Debris was starting to become evident on the mine floor. They reached section 14 and shined their lamps inside. There seem to be a haze in the lamp light. "Stay close," Jack whispered.

*Crack . . . pop*, Jack grabbed Matthew and pushed him hard against the opposite wall of the mine, a little further down the path, just as a thousand-pound sheet of coal dropped from the ceiling between the two men. This was followed a rain of small marble-sized and gravel-sized bits of coal with more dust.

Jack's voice rang out, "Father, are you OK?"

Matthew replied, a little shaky, "I'm ok, but I think the impact with the wall damaged the hand lamp."

"Don't move . . . stay next to the wall near the support. It's the safest place." Jack coughed, "Let this dust clear a little. Look up at the ceiling with your helmet lamp. Does the ceiling look solid like in other parts of the mine, or do you see cracks or separations?"

Matthew peered up to the clearing air toward the ceiling. What looked like large staggered slices of rock and coal hung between him and Jack. He continued to survey the ceiling above his own head and on down the path in section 14. "Jack, the ceiling looks like layers of playing cards between you and me and over my head."

"Not good," Jack came back. "How's it look on past your point in the tunnel?"

Matthew swiveled his gaze back down the tunnel. "It looks more solid, like the earlier part of the ceiling."

"Ok, here's what I want you to do, very carefully move further down the tunnel to where the ceiling looks better, not like the playing cards. But don't disturb anything. If you do, you could bring all of that down on top of you. I'm going to try and make my way down this side, along the wall. The ceiling looks solid where I'm standing, so you move first. Get to another support and stay along the wall."

"Alright, I'm going." Matthew moved on slowly trying not to lose his footing on the ever-increasing ceiling debris on the floor. It seemed to take forever to grope along with only his helmet lamp. Matthew had to stop a number of times and look at the ceiling to see if the playing cards were still there. Finally, the ceiling started to look more normal, the way it had earlier in the tunnel. "I'm clear," called Matthew to Jack.

"Good. Now find a wall support and stay close to it," Jack returned. "Give me a few minutes, I'll have to maneuver past this section of ceiling that fell, before I can make my way down to where you are."

Just then there was a deep rumbling, something one heard but also felt. Matthew jumped back against the wall where the next support stood. Then with what seemed like an explosion, the ceiling released its grip. The dust was blinding and difficult to breath. Slowly the dust started to settle. Where he had been standing a moment before was a solid mass of coal and rock.

Matthew took a deep breath and called out, "Jack, can you hear me . . . are you there?"

Silence.

Matthew looked around and found a fist-size rock, picked it up, and started banging it on the new rock wall that had been the passage. After several strikes Matthew stopped and listened, still nothing. Matthew dropped the rock, and it clattered to the floor with the other ceiling debris. Matthew started wiping at his eyes. The coal dust had been collecting on the moisture of his eyelids. He realized what he was doing and stopped before rubbing the coal dust into the eye itself.

Groping around in the coverall pockets he found a handkerchief and carefully wiped the coal dust from around his eyes, nose, and mouth the way he had heard the miners describing what they did numerous times a day. He shoved the handkerchief back into one of the pockets and started to survey his surroundings.

Black was the only thing that could describe his tomb. There were places on the wall where the light barely reflected, giving the false sense of a pocket or hole. Matthew reach out several times to explore the opening to find that it was solid. Matthew looked up. This part of the ceiling looked like it was more solid, which made him feel a little more secure. He continued to look around and listen. The path he was following still looked clear. He thought that there might be an intersecting tunnel which would allow him to cross to another tunnel to get out. So, Matthew, very carefully and staying next to the wall, proceeded down the dark path.

As Matthew probed the darkness, checking floor and ceiling as he went, started to think about Pappy's ordeal. For some reason, he felt a degree of comfort that he was not restricted in a confined pocket but able to move around.

Very quietly Matthew started to pray, "Lord Father, I need your guidance and strength. I know you created the Earth, the heavens, and all creatures. And no matter where we are, I know you can hear our prayers. Shine your light on the path you will have me walk. I feel like there is more for me to do, so I ask You to deliver me from this grave. Please, Father, hear this prayer, Amen." Matthew took a few more steps and saw it.

The passage was blocked by another collapse. But this seemed to be part of the wall and the ceiling. And the debris was smaller in size, not like the massive piece of stone which had sealed him in the tunnel. After making a lengthy inspection of the ceiling and walls, Matthew started removing some of the small chunks that were next to the solid wall. As he pulled more stones away, others would start to shift and fall from the ceiling-high pile. At one point, there was a considerable amount of shifting in the debris wall. There was enough movement that Matthew backed away to see what would happen. The stones shifted twice and then settled into their new jumbled order.

At this point, Matthew start to smile and shook his head. The pile of stones reminded him of a game he used to play in the orphanage where he grew up. He and the others would collect twigs about the length of a man's hand and drop them into a pile. Then each kid would try removing a twig from the pile without disturbing the other twigs. He had been fair at the game when he was younger, but the older and bigger he got the more difficult it was to retrieve a twig. With the game in mind, Matthew took a little more care in removing the next rock. He was going slower, but there was much less movement from the other stones.

After a while, Matthew was becoming rather warm and realized that since there was no air movement and he was doing so much activity, there was no breeze to cool him. Matthew sat back and studied the area he had excavated, trying to decide what to move next when he saw a few rocks next to the wall move on their own. Even more, he thought he saw a few thin beams of light between the stones. He quickly turned off his lamp, and sure enough, there was light struggling to get through. Matthew switched back on his lamp and started removing more rock.

Matthew started calling, "Jack, is that you?" He listened and thought he heard voices. "Boy, I thought I was going to be trapped for days."

Matthew stopped and listen. There were several voices along with the sounds of scraping and shifting pebbles. Just then about a six-inch section of the debris along the wall fell away and light streamed through. This was followed by a hand. Matthew grabbed it and shook it like it was a long-lost friend. Matthew let go and the hand disappeared back through the hole in the debris wall.

"Hallo," called a voice. "Who's there?"

Matthew hesitated; it didn't sound like Jack.

"It's me," Matthew replied. Matthew got close to the hole trying to see to the other side.

Then a light appeared, blinding Matthew. "Who are you . . . wait, it can't be, . . . Father Brooks?" said the voice with great surprise.

"I'm afraid so," said Matthew as he shielded his eyes from the lamp. "And who has come to rescue me?"

"Rescue you? We thought you were here to recue us!" continued the voice. "Is anyone with you?"

"No, just me. Jack Williams was with me. But we were separated, and a section of ceiling collapsed blocking the tunnel. I was hoping this was a way out."

"I hate to tell you, but there's only ten feet of tunnel beyond this pile of rubble. Me and the lads have been digging to try to get back to the main tunnel." Both sides of the wall fell silent as the reality of their combined situations sunk in. "Well, Father, I guess we should introduce ourselves. This be Ben Davies, and I have Seth and Samuel Evans with me."

"Are you all right?" inquired Matthew.

Ben answered, "Seth and I are ok. Samuel got a little banged up, scrapes and bruises mainly. He caught the edge of the cave-in but nothing serious. And you, Father; are you ok?"

Matthew said, "I'm fine, not a scratch." The conversation was replaced by the sound of a deep guttural rumble. There was a little coal dust settling down through the air, but that was all. After a few moments Matthew continued, "Any idea when things will settle down?"

Ben answered, "It's hard to tell. Sometimes the shifting can continue for a few minutes, and other times it could be days. We were doing an inspection of this section when . . ." Another rumble, like the groan of a giant, came oozing through the walls, floor, and ceiling. The low rumble died away. "Father," Ben continued, "I've never experienced anything like this, and the twins here with me are a little on edge." Another slight rumble groaned in the rock.

Then bang, a section of wall across from Matthew leapt out in a shower of fragment. Matthew raised his arm to cover his face and fell back against the wall where he had been talking to Ben. For a moment, all Matthew could hear was the rattling sound of rocks falling in place. But as that died out, Matthew heard a new sound, that of someone groaning. Suddenly Matthew realized it was himself.

Ben called out, "Father, are you alright? Are you hurt?"

Matthew answered, "I think so. I mean I'm ok, but I can't move my left leg. I seemed to be pinned by the rocks." Then a searing pain raced up his body to his brain. "Ohhh, I might be a little more than pinned."

Ben asked, "Can you see how you're pinned?"

"No, I'm half buried up to the waist in smaller rubble. Whatever has my ankle and foot is under the rubble." Then there was another cracking sound, a little muffled and he heard yelling. "Ben, what's happened?"

A few seconds later, coughing and through a choked voice Ben said, "Our section of tunnel has collapsed further. Samuel and Seth are up against the debris wall with me. It looks like we are now in a broom closet on this side."

Matthew could hear the twins since they were crowded around the small opening. "Father, can you get us out?" asked one of the twins.

"I'm afraid the Father is in no shape to help us right now," explained Ben.

"We're not going to make it, are we?" another voice asked.

Matthew heard the panic in the voices. He shifted around as best he could and shoved his hand through the hole, almost up to his shoulder. "Ben, take my hand. Samuel and Seth, one of you take Ben's hand, and the other take your brother's hand. Hold tight. I promise I won't let go no matter what happens."

One of the twins asked, "Father, would you say a prayer? The Miner's Prayer," the other added.

"Alright." Matthew cleared his throat, which was becoming dry from all of the coal dust.

> Each day I descend into the hole
> To earn my living digging coal
> I pray to my Father in heaven above
> That I may return to those I love
> If somehow death I should meet
> I want to wake at Jesus' feet
> I want my loved ones to be sure
> That in His arms I am secure

Matthew coughed. "Amen."

"Thank you, Father," he heard Ben say.

Matthew lay there in the silence, and then a thought came to mind. "Ben, do you know who wrote the Coal Miner's Prayer? I never did ask Father Griffith," Matthew asked.

"I have no idea," replied Ben. "I first remember hearing it from my granddad. He and my grandma would say it before he left the house for his shift in the mine. I've heard several different versions of the prayer over the years."

The rumbled started again, and this time it sounded as though it was angry. More debris started falling, but from where, Matthew couldn't tell. It seemed like it was coming from everywhere. He heard someone on the other side of the wall yelp and holler. Matthew took his free arm and covered his face from the debris that was falling. He felt Ben's grip tighten as the same happened with his. Matthew kept telling himself, *I can't let go, I can't let go.* The rumbling continued and became louder. The debris was starting to crush the air out of Matthew, but there was no way he could turn or shift to alleviate the pressure.

Then everything went black.

# CHAPTER 4

Hey, Matthias. Come on, we've been summoned. Here, take my hand. I'll help you sit up."

Matthias's head was swimming. He felt a firm grip in his hand which he returned. The next thing he realized, he was sitting up on the edge of a wood frame bed with a straw mattress. The stone floor was cool on his bare feet. He glanced up in the dim light and saw a strong angular face and dark hair, and he knew his name, Gaius! But when he tried saying something all that came out was a brief gurgle with a sharp pain that made Matthias wince.

Gaius said, "Wait, I'll get the physician. Be right back."

Matthias looked at his surroundings. His head was swimming. So many confusing thoughts. He was in a stone-built room where a number of beds such as his were around the perimeter of the room. Every so often, there were oil lamps mounted to the wall. The lamps had been burning for a long period of time, judging by the blackened marks up the wall and ceiling directly above the lamp flame. Opposite of himself, what seemed to be about forty feet away was a desk and stool with its own oil lamp.

Gaius was talking to the man sitting at the desk. The man had a dress, no, a toga draped about him. And Gaius was wearing some sort of long shirt with a segmented leather skirt and some form of upper body armor partially covered by a dark colored cape. Hanging from his side was a sheathed short sword.

Questions started racing through his head. He realized there was a coarse, dark, woolen blanket laying in his lap. He noticed he was bare-chested and only wearing some form of wrapping for shorts. At the foot of his bed, on another stool, was a neatly folded, light-colored garment and more leatherwear similar to Gaius's.

How did he know Gaius's name? Moreover, he seems to be remembering a number of things the longer he sat on the edge of the bed. But it was all confusing, he was in a coal mine, and he was in trouble, trapped. And his ankle was. . . . He moved a hand down and felt his ankle; it was perfectly all right. The confusing thoughts began to fade with his current situation coming into focus. Next, his hands moved up to his neck where he discovered a wrapping covering his throat. Lightly probing the covering, he felt a soreness roughly where his Adam's apple was located.

About that time the man sitting opposite in the room jumped up and rushed over to Matthias. "Here, here leave that alone. I just got the swelling down. I don't need to have you undo all I have accomplished the last day and a half," urged the physician.

Gaius seemed to be continuing the conversation he had been having with the physician. "As I said we have been summoned by Governor Pilate. Matthias and I must present ourselves. You said that the injury was not serious, that he would be fine."

The physician wheeled on Gaius, "I said he might be fine. Being struck in the throat can be fatal, but I think he is past the worst since the swelling has reduced. As to whether he will be able to talk again, only time will tell." The physician shifted his focus to Matthias, "You have to let your throat rest, if you ever hope to speak again. And that bump on your head is superficial. But if you leave the infirmary, I cannot be held responsible for the health of an *optio*." The physician turned back to Gaius, "Centurion Gaius, he will be your responsibility. He is to only drink liquids, slowly, in small quantities. Anything else could choke him and make matters worse. Do you understand me?" The glare from the physician was ice cold.

Gaius nodded and returned the stare. Without moving his head or breaking the stare, "Matthias, are you with me?"

Matthias reached up and grasped Gaius's forearm and raised himself to his feet.

The physician broke away from the stare, "Alright I will get an attendant to aid Optio Matthias in dressing." The physician raised his hand and motioned to another corner of the room. A young lad materialized from the darkness and approached. The physician motioned to the stool with the clothing and then to Matthias, "Assist the optio. He and the centurion have an appointment with Pilate. Be quick, but take care of the wrapping around his throat."

Matthias sat back down on the bed with a little help from Gaius. The attendant deftly slipped the tunic over Matthias's head and adjusted it around the neck. He then made the sandals materialize from around the corner of the bed. Once the sandals were laced into place, Gaius helped Matthias to his feet, so the tunic could be extended to its full length. The attendant next placed the leather stripped skirt about Matthias's waist with the empty scabbard. The physician was holding the leather vest and handed it to the attendant. Once the vest was in place, Gaius was holding the combination chest and back plate.

"Careful," urged the physician.

Both Gaius and the attendant slipped Matthias's right arm between the armor and fastened the left side together, encasing Matthias in the armor. Finally, a cape was produced and attached to loops on the upper shoulder points on the chest plate. The physician started to protest again but was silenced with another glaring stare from Gaius.

"Where's the optio's helmet?" Gaius ordered.

The attendant reluctantly retrieved the helmet from the next bed.

The physician explained, "We did not have time to send it to the armory for repair. We were too busy with the optio." The helmet had a creased dent above the right temple. "When the optio was struck in the throat he fell, and his head struck the edge of the wall. This is what had been reported to me when he was brought in. If it wasn't for the helmet, you may have been beyond any aid I could provide."

"These zealots, I've just about run out of patience," Gaius remarked under his breath and seemed to tense up.

Gingerly, the attendant placed the helmet on Matthias's head and fastened the chin strap. Then, almost instinctively, Matthias raised his left hand to his hip, where the hilt of the short sword would be. Gaius spun to see the attendant holding the short sword in his open palms with the hilt toward Gaius. Gaius relaxed and accepted the sword from the attendant who averted his gaze and withdrew from the area to his place in the dark. Gaius handed the sword to Matthias, who skillfully inserted it into the scabbard with a final click.

"Now that's better," announced Gaius. "What would I do without my second in command? Physician, I will take the best of care of my optio, and gods willing, return him to you for a little more rest. But from the looks of him, I don't think that will be needed." Gaius turned and started out of the infirmary with Matthias dutifully behind him.

As they negotiated the passages, Gaius moved to one side of the hall and in a low voice said, "Don't worry, I'll take care of everything. And don't try to talk. If they find out you can't give orders, you may get discharged from the army with no pension. Then where would you be? Back in that little village we grew up in with no prospects. Besides, I promised your father, my uncle, I'd take care of you. And the way things are in this army, you're the only one I can trust. Do you understand?"

Matthias nodded his head.

"Good. If things get to be too much, let me know, and we'll get you back to the infirmary." Matthias nodded and gave Gaius a wry grin. "That's more like it. Ok, let's go."

As they entered the receiving chamber of the Antonia Fortress, one could feel the charged atmosphere. There in the center of the austere room was Pontius Pilate sitting behind a stone table. Pontius Pilate, thin and dark-skinned from the middle eastern sun. Years of military service had hardened a young lad into a stern, middle-aged, Roman man. But the weight of political service was showing on his face and posture.

A number of scrolls lay about amongst the other trinkets of Pilate's office. Behind Pilate's right side was General Atilius, displaying his usual scowl. In front of Pilate were two Jews, one rather well-dressed and the other his servant, based on his attire and position, a few feet behind the first. These two were silent and seemed weary. But back by the entrance and being restrained from entering were six or seven priests, probably from the Sanhedrin. They were making so much noise, it was difficult to hear what Pilate was saying to the two Jews.

Gaius stopped at the left end of the table and stood at attention, while Matthias mimicked his moves.

"Silence! Silence, or you will be removed by force." Atilius did not mince words.

Between the appearance of Gaius, Matthias, and two more guards at the entrance, the noise makers quieted, more in fear than for any kind of respect for Pilate. Pilate turned his attention back to the two Jews who had been silently waiting.

"You were saying . . ." offered Pilate.

"My name is Joseph, Joseph of Arimathea, and this is my servant Malic. I have come to petition for the body of Jesus, the Nazarene," relied Joseph.

Pilate inquired, "Is this man a relative of yours?"

"No," responded Joseph.

Pilate continued, "Then why do you want this man's body, if he's not a relative? Do you owe his family or the individual some type of debt?"

"A debt . . . of a sort. He was a dear friend who had taught me much about myself and others. I wish to honor him by placing him in a tomb I had recently completed for myself," Joseph added.

Before anything else could be said, the commotion restarted by the entrance. Pilate stood and leaned across the table, glaring in the direction of the entrance.

"I. Said. Silence! . . ." Pilate's words echoed around the stone room.

"Please, your excellency, a word," pleaded one of the robed figures.

"I recognize you," Pilate said as he sat back down. "Let that one come forward, but the others remain at the entrance. And if they cannot hold their tongues, I just might have them removed to assure their silence. Do I make myself clear?"

It was not clear if this was a threat to the unruly group at the door or instructions to the guards. But the words had their intended affect.

The indicated member of the group was allowed to pass and advance to the right side of the stone table. Oddly enough, when he reached his position, he took on the air of piety, without saying a word.

Pilate motioned, "What is it, Caiaphas?"

Gesturing toward Joseph, Caiaphas started, "We cannot allow the Nazarene criminal to be handed over to this man."

"Oh," replied Pilate. "Is there some mystic Jewish law stating a friend cannot bury a friend?"

Caiaphas shifted his footing, and some of the piety seemed to also diminish. "He's not to be trusted," began Caiaphas.

"This man, Joseph?" Pilate noted, motioning toward Joseph.

"No," countered Caiaphas.

"Then to whom are you referring?" asked Pilate, his eyes narrowing at Caiaphas.

"Well," stammered Caiaphas, "the Nazarene."

"The man is dead," exploded Pilate. "You stood here earlier today and demanded that he be put to death. You chanted with the rest to crucify him. Well, you got your wish, and you're still afraid of him?"

"Well, you see," inserted Caiaphas, "the Nazarene told the people that he would . . . he would . . ." Caiaphas struggled to say the words. "He would rise again on the third day," his voice slowing and trailing off. "He was a mad man, a heretic. He was stirring up the people."

Pilate dropped back down in his seat and stared at his hands. "I should have listened to my wife when she told me not to have anything to do with this," Pilate said as he rubbed at his hands as though he was trying to remove something.

"The Sanhedrin and I demand—"

Pilate cut off Caiaphas in mid-sentence.

"You have done more than enough demanding," countered Pilate. "I would not press my patience any further, if I were you." Pilate shifted his gaze back to Joseph, "Tell me of this tomb. Where is it, and how is it constructed?"

Joseph kept his eyes fixed on Pilate. "The tomb is located on the edge of the graveyard, part of the gardens. It is hewn out of the rock, large enough for one. The entrance to the tomb is shoulder high, and two can enter, side by side. There is enough room inside for four to stand and a shelf on the right-hand wall to place a body, originally myself. To cover the entrance, there is a circular stone that is my height plus a head taller. The stone is three hands thick. There is a narrow trench that the stone rolls in, to cover the entrance. There is a slightly deeper impression at the tomb entrance which the stone rests to seal the tomb. Last week, I watched as five stout men rolled the stone in place to check the fit. It took six, with some leverage, to move the stone back from the entrance. It was quite a struggle to witness."

Pilate sat there, contemplating.

Caiaphas took in a breath to say something, but Pilate held up his hand, which stayed Caiaphas's words.

"I see no harm in letting this man have the body of . . ." Pilate searched for the name.

"Jesus of Nazareth," offered Joseph.

"Yes, Jesus. I believe he said he was king of the Jews," mused Pilate.

Caiaphas blurted out, "He's no king of mine! . . . Your excellency, if this is to happen, would you at least place a guard on the tomb for the next three to four days?" he implored.

"You really believe that Jesus will rise from the grave?" Pilate questioned.

"We fear that his followers will come and remove the body and claim he has risen," explained Caiaphas. "This would further claim that he was . . . is the messiah. The people would not listen to the priests. It would be chaos. And the zealots could use this as a rallying point to turn the people against Rome . . . and you."

This struck a notable nerve with Pilate. He motioned to Atilius, who bent down to listen to Pilate. The two held a brief discussion which was not audible to the others in the room. At one point Atilius pointed over at Gaius and Matthias.

Gaius whispered out of the side of this mouth to Matthias, "This doesn't look good."

Finally, Atilius stood up straight, resuming his disapproving statue-like appearance. Pilate motioned to one side, and a scribe appeared from the shadow in the back of the room. Matthias had not realized that there were a number of servants and a few soldiers standing just back to one side, where the scribe had come from.

Pilate again whispered to the scribe some instructions. Pilate then pointed to the end of the table. The scribe collected a small scroll and a pen and started writing at the end of the table where Pilate had indicated.

The tension or curiosity in the room grew as the scribe finished his task and presented the writing to Pilate for his approval. Pilate studied the writing and waived the scribe away. He then took a stick of wax and held the end of the stick in the small oil lamp flame on his table. Just as the wax was about to drip, Pilate maneuvered the stick back to the scroll and dabbed near the bottom of the writing. Next, he took his right hand and pressed his signet ring into the wax. After he removed the ring from the wax, he took one last look at the document before handing it to Atilius.

Pilate then turned his attention back to Joseph and Caiaphas. "This is what we are going to do," started Pilate. "I am releasing the body of Jesus of Nazareth to Joseph of Arimathea."

Atilius motioned to the unseen group behind them, and another servant stepped forward from the shadows. Atilius handed the document to the servant and motioned to Joseph. The servant dutifully carried the document around the table and handed it to Joseph. He then returned back to his original place with the other servants.

Pilate continued, "This document needs to be presented to the crucifixion officer. This will allow him to give you access to the body of Jesus. You are to take the body directly to the tomb you described and place him inside. The tomb is to be covered with the stone and sealed by my guards. I will have a guard placed at the tomb for the next four days. Anyone approaching the tomb, without authorization from my guard, will be put to the sword. Will this be sufficient Caiaphas?"

Caiaphas shifted, "I would like to have the temple guards oversee the transfer of the body from the cross to the tomb to assure it is not liberated by his followers."

"Agreed, but only to guard. They are not to interfere with the removal or entombment," added Pilate.

"One other point . . . I would like to have the temple guard also stand with your guard," Caiaphas urged.

Pilate stood again with both hands still resting on the table.

Atilius started forward but stopped with only one step.

"Your temple guard may watch from afar, but if they come within twenty paces of the tomb, they will be swiftly met by spear or sword. There are no exceptions. Do I make myself clear on this point, Caiaphas?" Pilate pressed.

Caiaphas nodded and shifted his gaze to the floor.

"Your exultancy," Joseph inserted. "Tomorrow is the sabbath. There is not time to prepare the body before sundown. We can only do a temporary preparation and need to do a proper burial the day following the sabbath."

Caiaphas's head snapped back up and was about to protest when Pilate replied. "It will be allowed but under Roman guard supervision. Only three will be allowed in the tomb to tend the body. If there are any infractions, the tomb will be sealed as is, and there will be no further discussion or requests. You will provide the workforce to roll the stone back for entrance and to reclose the tomb. Those that move the stone may not enter, just the individuals who will complete the burial preparations. The Roman guard will then reset the seal. Do all understand?"

Pilate surveyed the room looking for any questions. But his gaze was received with some form or other of acceptance.

"Very well, Joseph, I suggest you proceed quickly, since there are but a few hours before dusk. I will have a detachment waiting at the tomb you described. Caiaphas, you have my leave and take your followers with you. And Caiaphas, this has been twice today we have held discussions. I suggest we don't see each other for a period of time." As Caiaphas turned and started to leave, Pilate added, "A long period would be preferable."

Caiaphas hesitated and then hurried to the entrance where the guards allowed him to join the rest of the Sanhedrin. There was a moment of hushed discussion, and then they quickly left.

Joseph and his servant gave a slight bow, turned, and headed toward the same entrance that Caiaphas had passed.

General Atilius motioned and gave a grunt to Gaius and Matthias for them to come forward and stand before himself and Pilate. Instinctively, they moved to the indicated position and came to attention.

"Centurion . . ." Pilate began and then glanced at Atilius.

"Gaius," added Atilius. "And I believe his optio, Matthias"

"Yes," continued Pilate. "Centurion Gaius, I want you to assemble a contubernium, meet this Joseph of Arimathea at this tomb he described, and assure the body of this man, that Caiaphas is so fearful of, is placed in the tomb. Do you know the location of the tomb he described?"

Grabbing the hilt of his short sword and standing more erect than before, "I believe I do. Not far from the south wall of the fortress."

"That is my understanding also," mused Pilate. "Once the body has been identified and placed into the tomb, see to it that it is properly sealed. Place two guards on post at all times. No one is to approach within ten paces. Anyone within ten paces are subject to your authority . . . lethal, if you so determine. Supplies will be sent to you prior to the morning and evening fortress guard changes. I expect you will be on post for three days. If further time is required, Atilius will send a change of guard. Once this task is complete, report back to Atilius. Let's see, there's one more thing . . ."

Pilate reached across the table to a hand-sized wooden block, picked it up, and studied to for a moment. "This has the signet of the quartermaster. I believe he uses this to seal packages and vessels for storage. This should be appropriate for sealing a tomb, and I don't think any of these Jews would know how to read it." And with emphasis Pilate continued, "And they better not get close enough to read it! Understood?"

Pilate thrust the block toward Matthias. Almost by reflex Matthias took one step forward, reached up, retrieved the block from Pilate, and took the one step back, returning to his original position.

"Oh yes, do not draw your contubernium from the fortress guard. We are thin enough with all of this unrest."

Gaius shoulders dropped, and he had a look of bewilderment. "If not the fortress guard, where shall I find the men?" asked Gaius, half speaking out loud.

Atilius rounded the table and got into direct line of Gaius, "It is not up to you to question Pilate. You are supposed to be a centurion, find them. Search the jail, the infirmary, the kitchen, or wherever. Your time is short . . . move!" Atilius barked.

# CHAPTER 5

Both Gaius and Matthias drew themselves to full attention, turned, and left the room at a quick step. Halfway down the hallway, Gaius stopped and halted Matthias.

"Alright, I need you to go back to the infirmary and see what we can get out of there. Since the physician knows you can't speak, he will be more patient with you trying to communicate that we need men. I'll go and check the jail and anywhere else I can find. Understand?" Mattias nodded. "Good. Meet me at the fortress south gate to the gardens. We need six more men. Get what you can. Go."

Matthias headed back to the infirmary. As he entered the physician saw him and stood up from his table.

"I knew you would be back," started the physician.

Matthias waved a hand in front of the physician, held up three and then four fingers, made a sweeping motion around the room, and then waved his hand in the motion to follow.

Matthias's message connected with the physician. "You want three or four of these men to come with you?" inquired the physician.

Matthias nodded.

"Out of the question. These men are here because—"

Matthias cut off the physician by holding up the palm of his hand. The expression on Matthias face said as much, also. Matthias pointed at the first bed.

The physician glanced at the man and back at Matthias. "No, he has a broken leg and cannot lean on it for another week."

Matthias pointed to the next bed.

"He was just brought in. It's Gnaeus Runius," the physician said in awe. "I've not had time to examine him, but they tell me he has been bewitched.

Someone like Gnaeus, who has been victorious at so many battles, to end up in a daze, no, a stupor, after witnessing a common crucifixion."

Matthias pointed to the next bed.

"That man is Lucius; he had food poisoning. He insists on sampling the local cuisine and other amenities the city has to offer. He's a little weak, but he could possibly go with you. By the way, what do you need these men for?"

Matthias waived the physician off and pointed to the next bed.

"This one will be no good to you. He has been unconscious for two days. I've tried a number of things to wake him, but nothing has worked. And I still don't know what's wrong with him. They found him just outside of the prison area, slumped against the wall."

Matthias motioned around the rest of the dimly lit room.

"There are no others," replied the physician.

Matthias stood for a moment, then pointed at the second and third beds, and made the motion that they were to come with him.

The physician sighed, "I do this under protest." He motioned to the shadow in one part of the room, and a couple of attendants sprung forward from the dark. "Help prepare these two to leave with the optio," directed the physician.

A few minutes later, the attendants had prepared Gnaeus and Lucius, who were now standing before Matthias. Gnaeus looked as someone who was gazing into a far-off land, and Lucius still looked a little pale but was standing on his own.

"You two are to follow the optio," the physician motioned to Matthias, "for your next assignment. Optio, they are now your responsibility."

With that, Matthias motioned to the two to follow. The three left the infirmary into the maze of passages in the fortress.

Soon they approached a doorway into a small, open courtyard. As most Roman things go, it was very plain, austere. On the far wall was a guarded gate leading out of the fortress. Along the walls were benches. Matthias motioned for the two to sit down against one wall that was in the shadows. But there were few shadows since the sky was heavily overcast. And it appeared to have recently rained.

Matthias started to walk back through the courtyard and almost stumbled into a waist-high post protruding from the center of the courtyard floor. There were two heavy iron rings attached near to the top of the post. Matthias stood there for a moment lifting one of the rings in its swivel.

This meant something, but his mind was still foggy. He noticed some-thing reddish brown was in amongst the cracks in the wooden post and between the stones in the courtyard pavement.

Just then, Matthias heard someone approaching. It was Gaius emerg-ing from one of the other entryways into the courtyard with two more soldiers in tow. Gaius instructed the two soldiers to sit next to Gnaeus and Lucius. He then walked over to Matthias and guided him to the other side of the courtyard.

"I pulled these two out of jail," Gaius softly spoke. "The one on the right is Julius. He shouldn't be a problem. Seems to be a gambler who likes to bet more than he has. But the other, Marcus, is a brawler. It seems he picked a fight with that big Damascus fellow that arrived last week. Surpris-ingly, he was about to win when the big fellow kicked him off of himself, and Marcus landed on the captain of the guard. Seems he thinks he has something to prove. We'll need to keep an eye on him. I stopped by the infirmary to see how you did. The physician explained everything to me. Needless to say, he was not happy. I did offer to have him come along with us to help fill out our company, but he quickly decided he had more work and no time to talk."

Matthias gave Gaius a broad smile. Matthias held up two fin-gers and shrugged.

"I know," continued Gaius. "I'll work something out."

Just then there was a commotion just outside of the south gate en-trance. Gaius looked over Matthias's shoulder, "I think an opportunity is presenting itself."

One of the gate guards ushered in two soldiers, who apparently had been having a rather good time in the city.

"Centurion," addressed one of the gate guards. "These two were part of the crowd control earlier during the trial, but they seem to think they are now off duty while everyone is still on post. Should I take them to the prison?"

Gaius looked at the two leaning against one another. If you would remove one the other would fall. "I'll take care of them; you may return to your post," instructed Gaius.

The gate guard returned to his post shaking his head.

Gaius turned to Matthias, "Next to the wall by the gate entrance is a bucket of water. Bring it over behind these two, and on my signal . . . you know what to do."

Matthias, again with the broad grin, walked off to his task.

"Gentlemen," Gaius addressed the two drunk soldiers. "I need you to remove your helmets and tell me your names. I like to see who I am talking to, and the light is waning."

The taller of the two said, "I just got ole Antonius helmet the right way on his head, and now, you want him to take it off?"

"Yes, that is correct. And what might your name be?" inquired Gaius.

"I'm Scipio of Greece," as he removed his helmet.

Just as the two had removed their helmets, Matthias approached from behind and raised the bucket to head height.

"Do you two know who I am?" asked Gaius.

Scipio giggled a little, and Antonius gave Gaius a blank stare.

With the nod of Gaius's head, Matthias dumped the contents of the bucket over their heads. Both men gurgled with surprise.

"Now that I have at least part of your attention," glowered Gaius, "listen up and listen good. I could bring you both up on charges of abandoning your posts."

Antonius blurted out, "But we thought we were finished, relieved of our duties!"

"Silence!" ordered Gaius. "Abandoning your post is the death sentence!"

Gaius paused, giving the reality of their situation time to sink in past all of the wine they had been drinking. From the look on their faces, Gaius knew that his words had registered and the wine was losing its grip on them.

"Now, we could proceed to the prison cells, and I could file a report to be given to Pilate." Again, he paused, seeing the terror creep over their faces. "But I'm in a hurry and don't have time to disturb the governor. So, you are coming with me to finish your duty. And if either or both of you sneak away before we're finished, your names will be before Pilate so fast you won't have time to blink. Do I make myself clear?"

Both men straightened to attention or at least some semblance of attention. Scipio asked, "Sir, earlier you asked us who you are. Who are you?"

Gaius grimaced so as not to burst out laughing, "I'm Centurion Gaius. Do you think you can remember that?!"

Both men nodded, wide-eyed.

"Good! Replace your helmets and get over with the others."

During the discussion, Matthias had returned the bucket to its original location and returned to one side of Gaius. As the two men placed their helmets on their heads, some of the water from the original dousing had been captured and was once again pouring over their heads. This just added insult to injury, and the two sulked off to the benches where the others were sitting.

Gaius and Matthias turned their backs on the men, and Gaius stifled his laughter. "What a motley bunch. It's a good thing, we're not going into battle. Go over and bring me Gnaeus. If I can get through to him, I'm going to make him the *decanus* over the others."

Matthias nodded and proceeded over to Gnaeus. Gnaeus sat there, still with that distant look in his eyes. Matthias stood in front of Gnaeus and motioned for him to follow. Matthias might as well had been standing on the next continent. Matthias reached out and put his hand on Gnaeus shoulder to shake him. But as he touched him, Gnaeus stare broke, and he looked Matthias directly in the face.

"Did you see him? Did you hear him?" Gnaeus whispered.

At that moment something stirred inside of Matthias.

*Ben?* Matthew thought.

And then it was gone. Matthias motioned to Gnaeus to follow. Gnaeus stood and followed Matthias as one in a trance. Once they reached Gaius, Gnaeus stopped, and Matthias took his place next to Gaius.

"Roman soldier Gnaeus Runius, come to attention and look at me," ordered Gaius.

Gnaeus stood there with that distant stare.

"Gnaeus, you are a soldier of the seventh legion. I command your attention!"

Gnaeus seemed to respond. He was with Gaius, but he still looked like someone who had a question on their mind but couldn't quite figure out how to ask it.

"Gnaeus, I need you as my decanus. I need you to be responsible for these other five men," pointing in the direction of the others.

Gnaeus weakly responded, "Yes . . . yes sir." He seemed to straighten up a little, but he still had that puzzled look.

"Gnaeus, form up the men. We're moving out," directed Gaius. Gnaeus slowly turned and moved toward the others. Gaius added, "Matthias, you'd better help him assemble the men. I'll lead the way. You follow to make sure we don't lose anyone."

Matthias strode over and got the men up, placing them in a rank and file by twos. He then proceeded to the rear of the line.

Gaius announced, "You will follow me. Forward!"

And the group proceeded through the south gate of the fortress into the garden beyond, with Matthias following the column.

# CHAPTER 6

Judging by the shadows, what they were with this cloudy sky, Matthias figured that there was about an hour and a half of light left. The contubernium moved through the gardens with little notice of their surroundings. The particular path Gaius was leading along wound back and forth, allowing them to descend from the fortress and into the edge of the city's graveyard.

As they emerged from the gardens, Matthias noticed the contrast of living vegetation of the gardens with the desolation of rock piles. Everywhere one looked, the ground rolled and twisted with piles of rocks. Narrow paths could be seen weaving in and around the piles of stones. Occasionally an impression in the ground would be surrounded by stones, waiting for an occupant.

Gaius led them on a path that skirted the desolation on one side and the garden of life on the other. Eventually, the contubernium snaked its way back into the perimeter of the garden. Gaius raised an arm, and the little column of men came to a halt. Matthias moved from the rear of the group, up to Gaius's side.

Gaius pointed, "I think that's it."

It was a clearing backed by a solid stone outcropping that rose above the tree tops. In the side of the rock face was carved an opening as described by Joseph of Arimathea. Next to the opening, slightly elevated on an upward slope, was the massive round stone. It was impressive. Only a rich man could afford such a tomb compared to the piles of rocks just beyond the garden. Off to one side was a flat slab of stone, slightly elevated, big enough to hold a chariot and a full team of horses.

"That's where we'll make our camp," instructed Gaius. "It's close to the tomb, gives a clear view of the tomb entrance, control of access to the garden path, and an oversight of the common grave area. Gnaeus," called Gaius.

Gnaeus broke rank and approached Gaius.

Gaius noticed that Gnaeus seemed a little more aware of his surrounding and less in his stupor. "Gnaeus, I want you to take the men up on that slab of stone and allow them to rest until the Jews arrive with the body. While we wait, lay out a schedule for a watch on this tomb. I want two soldiers on post at all times. Plan for a rotation of every two hours at night."

Gnaeus clutched his sword hilt, straightened a little and responded, "Sir." With that he turned and returned to the men. Following his orders, Gnaeus moved the men onto the stone table where they either sat on the edge of the stone or laid down.

Gaius, looking around, "I hope our supplies arrive before dark. I'll feel a little better when we have a few watch fires built to assure no one can approach without being seen."

"Sir," Gnaeus standing on the stone table and pointing back the direction they had come from the fortress. An individual was leading a heavily laden donkey and accompanied by two soldiers with spears.

"Excellent! Take charge of the supplies, set up the camp, and set two watch fires. One over to the left of the tomb, about twenty paces, and the other here at the edge of the graveyard. Also, place the campfire there, near the edge of the table," directed Gaius.

Just then, Matthias saw the burial procession. They approached from the opposite direction than the soldiers had arrived. He could see Joseph of Arimathea and his servant leading the procession, with the servant following just behind and to the right of Joseph. Behind those two were eight men, four on either side of a blanket or sheet they carried between them. Behind the bearers were four women carrying rolled up cloth and small containers of various shapes and sizes. And bringing up the rear of the procession were five guards with spears.

Matthias grabbed Gaius's shoulder and pointed to the group that was now working its way around the edge of the graveyard to the garden area.

"Matthias, go and bring two of the soldiers over here with us. I have no concern with the burial party, but the temple guards need to know their place . . . and it's not here." Matthias gave a curt nod, spun on his heals, and headed for the makeshift encampment.

Matthias arrived at the campsite seeing most of the men moving supplies and setting up fires, all except for Scipio and Antonius. They were both leaning against some rocks off to one side, apparently staying out of Gnaeus's line of sight. It looked like their earlier celebration was wearing off.

Matthias approached Gnaeus, who snapped to attention. Matthias pointed to the two soldiers and motioned that they were to follow him. Gnaeus saw Scipio and Antonius, who had realized they had been caught.

Gnaeus raised his voice and issued sharp orders, "You two, here . . . now!" Scipio and Antonius hustled themselves over to Gnaeus and came to attention. "From this point on, I'm going to keep a special eye on you two. Just get out of line one more time and you won't have to worry about Gaius. He won't have a chance to get ahold of you; because when I'm done, there will be nothing left. Do I make myself clear!"

Both soldiers straightened to attention, clasped their sword hilts, and barked back, "Yes sir!"

"You two are to follow the optio. And by the way, the optio is an officer of few words. If he has to say anything to you, it may be the last thing you hear." Gnaeus turned his back on the two soldiers to face Matthias. "The men are ready, sir," Gnaeus announced and then gave Matthias a wink.

Matthias nodded and allowed a brief smile to rise and then fall from the left side of his mouth. Gnaeus stepped back and to one side. Matthias motioned to the two soldiers to follow, turned, and headed back to Gaius. The two soldiers promptly fell in behind and followed Matthias.

As Matthias and the two soldiers arrived, it appeared that Gaius was having an argument with the temple guards. The others in the burial party were quietly waiting off to one side. Matthias and the two soldiers stopped just behind and to the right of Gaius. As they stopped, Matthias grabbed the hilt of his sword and slapped the sword sheath against his side. With this Gaius knew there were four Romans facing the five temple guards, who now appeared to be a little less sure of themselves.

"As I was saying, you are not needed here. Return to your masters," announced Gaius.

The lead guard argued back, "But we were told to help guard the body. We will stand by the tomb and—"

Gaius cut the guard off, "Your services, what they might be, are not needed here. Once the body is in place and the tomb sealed, Roman soldiers will stand vigil. Pilate made the conditions of our presence very clear to Caiaphas and the Sanhedrin. I and my optio were present for the discussion. And before you leave, one other thing you should know, the guards positioned at the tomb entrance will have orders to stop, with whatever force needed, anyone approaching the tomb. If I were you, I would not come within say fifty paces, or your next resting place will be over there," motioning to the desolate rock mounds of the graveyard.

Gaius turning his head but keeping his eyes on the temple guards, "Soldiers of Rome."

Matthias and the other two reached across themselves with their right hands and clutched their sword hilts, and with their left hands grabbed the sword sheaths.

The lead temple guard retreated a step and then two. The other guards looked like they were ready to bolt. The lead guard motioned to the others to back away, not taking his eyes off of Gaius.

The three Roman soldiers stood there motionless.

The temple guards all backed away, the way they had come until they were a good thirty paces. They turned and huddled for a moment and then moved off further. About sixty paces away, two of the guards took up positions on either side of the path while the other three disappeared down the path, probably going back to report to Caiaphas.

Gaius turned to Matthias and the two soldiers and motioned for them to relax. "I don't think we'll have to worry any more about them. But to be sure, the two of you," pointing to Antonius and Scipio, "stand guard here. Let me know if anyone comes down this path. Optio, you're with me." With that Gaius and Matthias moved off to the burial party while the two soldiers took up their positions at the path.

Gaius and Matthias approached Joseph, who was talking with others in the burial party. One of the bearers noticed Gaius and Matthias approaching and let Joseph know, who turned to face the Romans.

"May we proceed? The hour is late, and there is not much time left before the sabbath," said Joseph.

The calmness with the way Joseph spoke caught Gaius off guard. "Um yes, but remember, only three of you in the tomb at a time," reminded Gaius. "Pilate's orders."

"I don't think that will be a problem. There's not much more room than for three," responded Joseph.

Gaius and Matthias stepped back to watch the proceedings.

Joseph's servant first entered the tomb and lit a couple of oil lamps with a small lamp he was carrying. The inside of the tomb had a soft glow, and Matthias could see back into the tomb. On the right side of the tomb, there appeared to be a shelf carved into the wall, large enough for a person of Joseph's height.

Once Joseph's servant completed his task he walked out of the tomb and took his place next to Joseph. Next, two of the bearers positioned themselves, one at the head and the other at the foot of the body that was laying on the blanket. The other bearers positioned themselves along the sides of the body, three on each side. The one at the head of the body entered the tomb first, walking backwards. As each of the bearers came to the edge of the tomb entrance, they released the blanket and stepped back to the sides until only the bearer at the foot of the body remained, until he too entered the tomb. At this point, the women started moving toward the entrance.

Gaius raised his hand and was about to say something when Joseph intervened. "A moment," Joseph said to the women and looking back at Gaius.

Gaius held up three fingers.

"Mary, take the shroud linen in and leave it with the bearers. They know what to do," instructed Joseph. The woman carried the linen bundle into the tomb and handed the material to one of the men. She hesitated for a moment, looking at the body, and then quickly left the tomb and joined the other, quietly sobbing.

"Centurion!" called Scipio from his position on the path.

Gaius told Matthias, "Go see what that's all about."

Matthias left the tomb and went to see what was happening. As he drew closer, there were three men, one wearing what looked like the robes of the Sanhedrin and the other two looked like servant class, both carrying clay containers. When Scipio realized it was Matthias approaching, he came to attention. Matthias pointed at the robed figure.

"My name is Nicodemus. I am a Pharisee. I bring myrrh and aloes for the burial. May we deliver them to Joseph of Arimathea?" Matthias stood there for a moment then motioned for the three to follow. He noticed as they started walking to the tomb Scipio seemed to relax a little, but when Matthias turned to look back down the path, Scipio straightened back up.

Matthias led the three to Gaius, who was standing next to Joseph. Several of the bearers and the women tensed up as the robed figure approached. Joseph was the one who intervened as the bearers moved toward Nicodemus.

"Why have you come?" questioned Joseph.

"I bring myrrh and aloes for the burial," offered Nicodemus. "Please accept these from one who has spoken on Jesus' behalf in the past."

"I have heard of this. Were you not the one who challenged the Sanhedrin earlier concerning trying Jesus of Nazareth in his absence?" inquired Joseph.

"Yes," responded Nicodemus. "I had several conversations with Jesus in the last several months. He did not deserve this. Caiaphas and the rest of the Sanhedrin are afraid of him. Even now, they are holding council. Arguing amongst themselves on what should be done next."

"Was he your friend?" asked Joseph.

"I hoped he had considered me his friend. One night he told me that I needed to be born again. I didn't understand. I'm old, and death is closer to me than birth. He also told me during our discussions that the Son of God was not sent here to judge us, like the judges of old, but to save us. Everything is very confusing. And now," motioning toward the tomb, "his saving anyone seems impossible." Nicodemus seemed to grow older and distant in his thoughts.

"Please leave the burial preparation here. I will see that they are placed in the tomb over the Sabbath. There is not enough time to complete the burial preparations. We will come back and finish after the Sabbath," offered Joseph. Nicodemus nodded and motioned for the two bearing the clay vessels to place them on the ground. As Nicodemus turned to leave, Joseph added, "Peace be with you."

Nicodemus hesitated for a moment, nodded again, turned, and left without another word. The two servants followed him back down the path.

Gaius asked, "What do you mean that you'll finish the burial after the Sabbath?" to Joseph.

Joseph pointed over to the west, "The sun has almost set. We can do no work on the Sabbath, which is drawing near. We need to finish up and close the tomb before sundown. We would like to return after the Sabbath and finish anointing and wrapping the body . . . of course with your permission."

Gaius looked to the west, shifted his stance, and glanced back at the tomb. "Alright, but only bring those needed to finish the burial preparations."

Joseph reminded, "I also need to bring enough men to remove the stone and replace it once we are done."

"Yes, of course. But make it mid-morning. I want plenty of light to view the proceedings," answered Gaius.

"We will conform to the conditions, and I am personally grateful for your indulgence," offered Joseph.

"It looks like we're about finished," as the two bearers emerged from the tomb. "Please place the remaining items the women are holding and these two clay vessels in the tomb." The two bearers and one other collected the items and carried them into the tomb. Upon their exit from the tomb, the men started to assemble themselves by the great round stone to seal the tomb.

Gaius held up a hand and spoke to Joseph, "Would it be allowed for myself and my optio to view the body before sealing the tomb?"

Joseph looked a little concerned.

Gaius continued, "I mean no disrespect, but I'm expecting Pilate to question me as to assure the placement of the body. I'd appreciate it if you would join us."

Joseph mused on this for a moment, nodded, and then motioned for them to follow.

Matthias followed Gaius, who in turn was following Joseph. Matthias noticed the smoothness of the stone opening as he bent and passed into the tomb. Surprisingly, the few lamps in the tomb provided ample light.

The craftmanship of the opening was surpassed with the interior of the tomb. The walls were smooth, no signs of chisel marks. And the temperature was noticeably cooler inside. But the most notable thing was the odor of the ointments and other burial preparations. In the wall was the carefully carved niche, where the body lay. Fresh linen draped over the body and more linen lay folded at both the head and feet, in preparation to complete the burial.

Gaius reached toward the corner of the shroud near the head.

Joseph shifted and asked, "Is it really necessary?"

Gaius nodded, "Yes, I need to see the face to assure it is him."

Joseph asked, "Did you know him . . . Jesus?"

Gaius hesitated and then pulled the corner of the shroud back to expose the body to the shoulders. "I met him a couple of years ago when I was in Capernaum, in need of someone who could cure an ailing servant. I also saw him when he was first brought to Pilate, before he was sent to Herod." Gaius stopped and just stood there.

The man who lay in the niche was well lit by the lamplight, and yet, he almost was unrecognizable. Even though the body appeared to have been washed, blood was caked in his hair and beard. His face was swollen and discolored. Across the brow there were a small row of holes. In a few of the red holes, a spot of white could be seen, bone. Overall, his skin was pale, very pale from the loss of blood. There were lash marks just visible around the shoulders leading to the back.

Gaius quickly pulled the shroud back over the mutilated face and adjusted the linen back, so it lay as before. He turned to Joseph, who had averted his eyes. "I'm sorry Joseph. I had heard that he had been scourged and beaten, but I had no idea it was to this extent. If I had not seen him early this morning, I may not have been able to recognize him. We can leave now."

Matthias turned and exited the tomb. Joseph quickly followed Mattias, and Gaius emerged last.

Joseph went over to his servant and said something to him, but Matthias could not quite make out the instructions. The servant quietly maneuvered past Gaius and disappeared into the tomb. Before Gaius could say anything the light in the tomb began to dim, and then the tomb was dark. The servant emerged from the black opening of the tomb and returned to Joseph's side.

"With your permission, centurion, it is time," announced Joseph.

Gaius nodded and stepped back from the tomb opening.

Without another word, the eight men who had originally borne the body to the tomb deftly moved to position themselves around the massive round stone. In unison, seven of them rocked the stone backward as the eighth man removed a small stone which held the monolithic door in place. Once the stone was removed, the eight strained and struggled as gravity pulled the round disk of stone down the groove to finally block the tomb entrance.

Gaius looked over at Matthias, "See if they sent a measure of wax or putty in our supplies. If so, bring it to me."

Matthias gave a sharp nod, turned, and headed to the encampment on the rock table. As he approached, Gnaeus saw Matthias and came to attention. Matthias motioned to Gnaeus to relax. Matthias then made a few motions with his hands as though he was holding clay and forming something. He then pointed at the pile of supplies.

Gnaeus first looked puzzled and then a thought struck him, "I think I know what you're looking for. I was wondering why they had sent that lump of potter's putty." Gnaeus went over to the pile of supplies and retrieved what looked like a wine skin, but it had a drawstring tied off on the top of the bag. Gnaeus returned to Matthias and presented the package. Matthias took it, nodded, and left the camp for the tomb.

When he returned, everyone was standing in silence. Gaius inspected Matthias's package.

"This should work," Gaius announced as he loosened the drawstring and allowed the round glob of moist putty to roll into his hand. He then went to the immense stone and placed the putty right at the joint where the stone door met the outer surface of the tomb. Gaius pressed and formed the ball into this joint about shoulder high. He then turned to Joseph's servant who was holding one of the oil lamps that had lit the tomb.

"I need to borrow this," as Gaius took the lamp from the surprised man's hands.

Everyone looked on in curiosity as to what Gaius was going to do next. Matthias had not noticed before, but Gaius had the signet of the quartermaster on a leather strap, attached to his belt. Gaius took the signet from his belt, studied it for a moment, and then tipped the opening of the lamp over the signet so that a trickle of oil fell on it. After coating the signet, Gaius handed the lamp back to the servant. Next, Gaius pressed the oily signet into the lump of putty and then withdrew the signet. Even though the light was starting to fade, the marking of the signet was clearly visible.

Gaius announced loudly enough so that the two remaining temple guards could hear, "This tomb is sealed and now under the protection of the Roman Empire by decree of Governor Pontius Pilate. This tomb will remain sealed until the day after tomorrow. At that time, only three will be allowed to enter to complete the burial preparations. The tomb will be resealed once the preparations are complete." And then with a little extra authority Gaius added, "Before the morning of the third day, anyone approaching this sealed tomb will be at risk of forfeiting their life."

Gaius stood there and surveyed the faces that were in front of him and the ones of the temple guards, at a small distance. At about the same time Gnaeus came stomping up with Lucius and Marcus in tow.

Gnaeus saluted Gaius, "Sir, the first posting of the guard!"

"Yes," responded Gaius, "post the men on either side of the stone."

Gnaeus turned to the two and pointed to the two locations and said, "Move!" Both soldiers deftly took their positions, each holding a lance.

Joseph motioned to the burial party to leave and briefly turned to Gaius. "I thank you. We will return the morning after tomorrow," and he added, "well after first light."

Joseph gave a nod to Gaius who returned the nod. Joseph turned and joined the burial party who had already started down the path past Scipio, Antonius, and the two remaining temple guards.

Gaius then turned to Gnaeus, "It is almost dusk, set the watch fires. Oh, and have those two," pointing back down the path, "come back to the camp. I don't think we need to guard the path any longer."

Gnaeus snapped to attention, grasp the sword hilt on this belt, and responded, "Sir!" Gnaeus moved off to retrieve Scipio and Antonius.

Gaius placed a hand on Matthias's shoulder, "Come on, let's see what the fortress sent us for dinner." The two walked back to the stone table en-campment. As they walked, Matthias heard Gnaeus giving orders to Scipio and Antonius to set up one of the watch fires.

# CHAPTER 7

Tomorrow, when the porters show up from the fortress, I want to have a word with them about our supplies," Gaius told the others that were sitting at the camp's fire. "There's no reason for us to eat field rations when the fortress is but a twenty-minute walk away. No matter what is going on in the morning, I want to be told when the porter arrives. He's not to leave until I've spoken with him."

With that Gaius tossed the remainder of the field ration biscuit into the fire and stood up. "Matthias, I think we need to check the area before retiring," Gaius said, picking up his helmet and replacing it on his head.

Matthias was sitting on a bundle of firewood that the porters earlier brought for the fires. He grabbed his helmet and stood up, slightly off balanced. He quickly recovered and paused to make sure he wasn't going to fall on his face.

Gaius watched with concern, "We'll make quick work of the inspection; then you can rest. That goes for all of you. You'll each be pulling watch shifts tonight."

Matthias walked over to Gaius, and they both walked off over towards the tomb.

As they approached, Marcus called out, "Halt and be recognized!"

"Stand down soldier," replied Gaius. "The optio and I are checking things out before retiring. Anything to report?"

"No sir," replied Marcus. "It's as quiet as a tomb . . . so to speak."

"Sir," added Lucius, "beyond the perimeter, down the path, I think I saw something . . . but I'm not sure."

Matthias strained to see down the dark path but could not make out anything in the dark past the perimeter fire. Gaius mused and then addressed Marcus, "Soldier, did you see or hear anything?"

"No sir, the perimeter fire was blocking my view," reported Marcus.

"I see," said Gaius. "The optio and I will check it out."

Gaius motioned to Matthias to follow. They walked as though they were walking out of the garden and into the stony cemetery. Once out of the firelight, Gaius whispered to Matthias, "Draw your sword just in case. I'll take the left side of the path, and you the right. Stay in the shadows. We'll go fifty paces. I'll step into the path and announce myself. You stay in the shadows, unless I call for you."

Avoiding the firelight, the two moved silently to either side of the path and started down. At thirty-eight paces down the path, Matthias could hear low voices talking. Jews, from the sound of it. Matthias could barely see Gaius, who had paused to listen. He heard them too. Gaius started moving, so Matthias did the same. At forty-seven paces Gaius halted.

There seemed to be a little light here because he could see Gaius better. He was motioning that the path was making a turn, and from his position, he could see something just around the turn. Gaius motioned for Matthias to stay and then held up his sword, signaling to be ready. Gaius took a few more paces and then stepped into the middle of the path.

Announcing himself, "My men have been watching you!"

Matthias heard startled voices, more Hebrew.

Gaius continued, "Need I remind you that if you approach my men, they have orders to strike first and ask questions later. I maintain, you need to stay away from the tomb."

More Hebrew, but it was difficult for Matthias to make out exactly was being said from his position on the path. Something about the Sanhedrin.

Gaius spoke slowly and clearly, "I don't care what your masters want. Caiaphas requested our presence to Pilate. Pilate has ordered his soldiers to stand watch, and that's exactly what we are doing." Gaius raised his sword and pointed at the unseen individuals. "You have been warned for the final time. Matthias, join me."

Matthias stepped up to Gaius's side, sword at the ready. Matthias saw four temple guards who had been sitting around an almost nonexistent fire. When Matthias appeared at Gaius's side the four recoiled a few steps back. Their swords and spears laid about the ground where they had been sitting.

"Need I bring more of my men forward to assist you with your departure?" Gaius added.

From the worried looks, Matthias could tell the guards were not sure exactly how Gaius meant when he referred to *their departure*. Cautiously, the guards retrieved their weapons and then hurriedly moved further down the path into the darkness.

After a moment, Gaius sheathed his sword; Matthias followed his example.

Gaius, still looking down the path, "I don't think we'll see any more of them tonight. Remind me in the morning, we'll send a couple of men down each path periodically tomorrow just to make sure. Come on let's head back to the camp."

They started walking back up the path.

"How's your throat doing? Try saying something." They stopped, and Gaius turned toward Matthias.

Matthias opened his mouth, but all would come out was a soft gurgling.

"That's enough, don't want you to strain anything. Give it some more time. It will be fine." The look on Matthias's face must not have been good. Gaius continued, "Cheer up, you know how the women like the big silent type. Yeah, I knew that would get a smile out of you. Don't worry you'll be fancy talking that pretty redhead in the market. Yes, I saw you last week talking to her. I'm not blind. And I could tell, she was all starry eyed over you. Come on let's get back."

As they emerged from the path, there was Gnaeus standing by the two posted guards. Gaius and Matthias walked over to the threesome.

"Sir, I was just about to check—" Gnaeus started before he was cut off.

"Everything is alright, Decanus," Gaius stated. "Lucius, is it?" referring to one of the soldiers. "Good man, there was someone down the path moving about."

Gnaeus shifted and looked down the dark path.

"It's ok, they were just temple guards . . . nothing to be concerned about. The optio and I sent them packing. I don't expect them back tonight. As a matter of fact, I don't expect much of anything tonight or tomorrow. It's their sabbath; things will be quiet."

"Sir, if I may," inquired Gnaeus, "how do you know it will be quiet?"

"You've not been here very long; what a week or two?" asked Gaius.

"I arrived ten days ago from Athens, and before that, I was in the Germanium region with the second legion," replied Gnaeus.

"Yes, I thought so," remarked Gaius. "The Jews hold their sabbath once a week . . . their day of rest. It's a day to worship their God."

Gnaeus frowned, "Which of the gods would that be?"

Gaius stood there for a moment then continued, "They only have one god. And as I understand it, the god has no name, but they do refer to the god as *him*. Anyway, on their day of worship, they are forbidden to do anything. No labor of any kind. I once saw a man's donkey stumble into a hole and could not get out. The man and a few others just sat there next to the hole, not doing a thing. I was very puzzled by this and asked the man why he was not helping the animal. He said it was the sabbath, and they would get the donkey out the next day. It's rather amazing how closely they follow their religious rules. But at the same time, there are these so-called temple guards always watching the people. And if they see something, they scurry back to their masters, the Sanhedrin, to report on the offender. Then the Sanhedrin have the offender brought to the temple and tried for their infraction. The people are afraid of the Sanhedrin, and so far, the Sanhedrin are afraid of Romans."

Gaius hesitated for a second as though he was trying to recall something. "I believe there is something special about this sabbath, I think they call it Passover. I'm not really sure what this Passover is, something that happened a long time ago. But they will be in their homes and at the temple. Even the markets will be closed. Not because there's a restriction, it's just there will be no one there to buy or sell. Even the foreign merchants take the day off, to count their money." Gaius motioned to Matthias, "The optio and I are going to turn in, the encampment is yours, Decanus."

Gnaeus came to attention, his hand on the hilt of his sword. "Good night, sir, all will be well."

"One would hope," replied Gaius.

With that Matthias followed Gaius back to the encampment. At the camp Matthias found a pile of folded blankets and took one. The night was starting to cool, which made Matthias start to think about where to bed down. Over by the fire there was a boulder at about the right distance to stay warm but not too warm.

Matthias walked over and dropped the blanket and removed his helmet. He set the helmet up on the boulder, which was about waist high. He looked around and saw Julius poking around in the supplies. At about that time, it appeared Julius found what he was looking for and started back to the fire. Matthias motioned to Julius to come over and help him remove his chest armor. Julius understood and moved around behind Matthias.

"Ready, sir?" Julius asked.

Matthias nodded and placed his hand on his chest plate.

Julius released the side strap between the back and chest plate on Matthias's left side and then pulled the tethered pins on the top of the armor on Matthias's shoulders. Julius then eased the back plate away from Matthias which allowed Matthias to slide out of the left side opening. Julius then set the armor down next to the boulder.

"Anything else, sir?" asked Julius.

Matthias shook his head no and gestured a thank you.

Julius turned to walk over to a spot he had already prepared for himself and said over his shoulder, "Good night, sir."

Matthias motioned again, but Julius's back was to him. Matthias finished removing his forearm gauntlets and his leather skirt with this sword. He laid all of these items next to the armor. He then sat down with his back to the rock and covered himself with the blanket. He sat there for a moment thinking he had forgotten something. He then reached over and pulled the sword out of its sheath and placed the sword next to himself, under the edge of the blanket.

Matthias sat there staring into the fire and thinking about the face of the man in the tomb. He had been beaten and tortured to the point where it was difficult to know who it was. But at the same time, there was a look of peace in that mutilated face. Like something had been accomplished, and all was well. Between the events of the day, the warm stone, and the cool night, sleep wandered in and carried Matthias off.

# CHAPTER 8

It was a restless sleep. At first the dreams were of green wooded land with numerous cool streams. He felt like the paths through the woods were ones he had walked before, familiar and yet very different. But then, the dreams started to shift to a dark, enclosed space. This too was familiar but not somewhere he wanted to be. He was reaching into a hole in the wall, something grabbed his hand, then the walls, floor, and ceiling started to shake . . .

Matthias awoke! Before him were the glowing embers of the campfire, and the sky was beginning to glow with the start of a new day. Not far away, he could see the two sentries standing guard on either side of the great round tomb stone. Others were starting to stir in the camp, and he heard a cock crow. Matthias sat there for a few moments trying to decide what was more real, the dream or what he was seeing.

Gaius stepped up beside Matthias from the side of the rock Matthias was sitting on. "Wouldn't you do better lying down to sleep?" questioned Gaius.

Matthias raised a hand to the wrapping on his throat.

"Let's see if a night's rest has made a difference. Try saying something," offered Gaius.

Matthias cautiously tried to speak, but again, only a muffled gargle passed from his lips.

"That's ok, old friend," assured Gaius. "After this, we'll ask for leave. Both of us could do with a little relaxation up at the spas in Tarsus. I know of twin Carpathian sisters we could visit. It would do you some good. Come on, get dressed. I want to have the camp in shape for when our breakfast and supplies arrive from the fortress. I'm going to find Gnaeus and see what the sentry schedule is for the today. As soon as you're ready, I want you to come with me to check up on our friends from the temple down the path.

96

I see them as being harmless, but I still don't trust them. Even swine will turn on their master, given half a chance." Gaius gave Matthias a pat on the shoulder and strode off in search of his decanus.

Within a short time, Matthias was suited up and had started stretching his legs around the campsite when Gaius reappeared.

"Good, let's take that walk," Gaius stated.

They first walked over to the tomb entrance to check on the watch. "Sentries, what is the condition of the post?" ordered Gaius.

Both soldiers snapped to attention, and Julius spoke up first, "Julius and Antonius on post, the tomb is secure, all is quiet."

Gaius turned his gaze to Antonius. "Anything to add soldier?" inquired Gaius.

"Only we have been on post for a short time. The decanus told us the night was without event, but we are to be weary with day break," replied Antonius.

"Very good, continue the watch. The optio and I are going to check on the temple guards, down the path," instructed Gaius. Gaius gave a glance to Matthias and motioned with a nod to the path. Both men turned and proceeded to the path while the posted guards remained at the tomb.

Gaius led the way, but Matthias was right by his side. The sun was up and was casting long shadows across the path. As they approached the bend in the path, Gaius slowed and then came to a stop. Gaius lightly tapped his ear, pointed down the path, and looked at Matthias with a questioning expression.

Matthias shook his head no.

Then they both quietly proceeded. As they came around the bend, they saw the abandoned campsite. Matthias walked over to the meager remnants of the campfire from the night before and held his hand near the remains. He stood up and shook his head.

"Well, I'm glad to see they took last night's warning to heart," said Gaius. Gaius could see another one hundred or so paces further down the path. "They probably moved down there, further . . . last night. Just as well, they'll be reporting back to the Sanhedrin that all is quiet, which will keep Caiaphas out of Pilate's ear. That will make things better for us. Come on, let's head back to camp. Hopefully, our supplies will have arrived. And the food better have improved, or there will be a dispatch sent to the captain of the watch telling him not to allow the bearer of our supplies back into the fortress until I have a few chosen words with them."

As they were walking back, Gaius seemed to be troubled.

"Yesterday, when we were in the fortress with Pilate and the others, Caiaphas was worried about the body being stolen from the tomb. He said something about a number of days," Gaius mused.

Matthias held up three fingers.

"Yes, three days. Well, with yesterday being the first day, today being the second, tomorrow will be the third day. We need to speak with Gnaeus and make preparations. If Caiaphas's fears are true and zealots try to take the body, they'll try either shortly after sunrise or just prior to sunset. I want everyone up before sunrise and prepared for an attack. I don't think they will come from the direction of the graveyard, it's too open . . . exposed. They'll have to come down one or both of the paths. We might be able to use the temple guards to our advantage."

Matthias stopped, placed a hand on Gaius's arm, and gave him a questioning look.

"No, not as fighting support but as a warning of someone approaching. If we allow the temple guards to make their encampment tonight part way down the path, anyone trying to sneak up from that direction will stumble upon the guards. The guards make so much noise trying to get out of whoever's way, we'll have a good minute's notice to prepare. Yes, we just need to make it look like it's their idea to camp closer."

And with that, the two men arrived at the stone table encampment. It appeared that the supplies had been delivered and the bearers had left.

Gnaeus approached and saluted Gaius. "Sir, I hope you do not mind, but I started the men not posted on breakfast. We will be changing the post soon and thought it would be better to change the post with fed men than those distracted with hollow bellies," reported Gnaeus.

"Good thinking, I approve," replied Gaius. "I would also like to discuss some strategy for defending the tomb." Gnaeus looked a little surprised. "I think we'll be fine for most of the day. It's tomorrow morning and tomorrow evening that concerns me. Today is the Jews' sabbath, their holy day. They are forbidden from doing anything that looks, sounds, or smells like work. You'll not see many of them today. Let's get something to eat and sit over there where we can discuss guard placements. By the way, I hope that something decent was brought to eat."

"Well, it's not from the emperor's personal kitchen, but I think you'll find what we have to eat more to your liking. At least the men seem to think your talk with the bearers last night had its desired effect," responded Gnaeus, with a bit of a grin.

The three retrieved fresh bread, still warm, from the bundles of supplies. They each took a pouch containing roasted goat. Matthias pulled from one of the packages three bronze bowls. He stood up with a quizzical look.

Gnaeus held up a wine skin and nodded at the bowls. "Well, I guess my talk with the porters did work," said Gaius.

The three proceeded over to the earlier designated spot and started eating.

Gaius reached over to the edge of the campfire, retrieved a bit of charcoal, and started making marks on the stone in front of him. "This, here, is the tomb," Gaius spoke as he drew. "The path leading back to the fortress is this line, and the path where the temple guards will be is here. This region is the rock cemetery out over there," waving his hand toward the desolate stony ground.

"And this is our encampment. Gnaeus, I want you to station the men. In the morning before sunrise, I want two at the tomb entrance, two at the entrance to this path," indicating the path to the fortress, "and two concealed to the sides of the path where the temple guards will be. The optio and I will position ourselves up on this stone table. We will be able to direct and reinforce any of the two path accesses, if attacked. We will also be able to monitor the cemetery, just in case anyone tries to approach from that direction. Gnaeus, you've been in a number of campaigns, and I realize this is nothing like those battles. But I would like your opinion on this strategy."

Gnaeus wrinkled his face a bit as he studied the layout. "It looks sound to me," started Gnaeus. "Every possible direction of attack is covered, you have the best vantage point, and a support plan. But I have a few questions, if I may, sir."

Gaius nodded.

Gnaeus continued, "If you're expecting an attack, shouldn't we request more support from the fortress, and why tomorrow morning?"

"No, I think we'll be able to handle a group of zealots," started Gaius. "For starts, they are unorganized and not trained fighters. We are well-armed. Their only advantage would be surprise, which is why I want to be prepared. And a couple of prepared soldiers can easily block, defend, and hold the attackers to these paths. They would have a difficult time trying to leave the path and move through all of the vines. We'd be able to pick them off one by one as they emerge. As for when they would attack, it would not be midday. They would be too easily spotted. They will attempt anything either at day break or at dusk. And today is their sabbath, umm . . . a day of rest and worship."

"This one god you told me about earlier?" asked Gnaeus.

"Yes," continued Gaius. "They may not attack, but I would prefer to be prepared."

"Would this have anything to do with . . ." Gnaeus's voice trailed off.

"With what?" pried Gaius.

"Well," Gnaeus hesitantly began, "during the execution of the one that lays in the tomb," gesturing to where the guards were posted, "there were murmurings amongst the onlookers that he would rise again from the grave."

Gaius looked concerning at Gnaeus.

Gnaeus continued, "At one point, the Jews started to argue amongst themselves about this. The Jews stopped arguing when one of the other condemned men, a thief I think, said something about he should save himself and the other two being executed. But then the other being crucified argued with the thief and told him to leave this man alone. That the two of them deserved what was happening but not him, the one the thief was . . . was tempting. All of the executions I have seen, I have never seen such . . ." Again, Gnaeus's voice trailed off, and he seemed to be slipping back into the state that he was found in the infirmary.

"Decanus," ordered Gaius, "do you have any other questions?"

This brought Gnaeus back to the conversation at hand. "Ah, yes sir. You chased the temple guards off last night. How do you plan to get them back and willingly participate in the tomb defense?"

Gaius smiled, "I don't expect them to willingly participate. As a matter of fact, I don't want them in the way of the fighting. They would be more trouble, and one of the men might get hurt. No, if the attack comes from this path," pointing at the charcoal diagram, "those temple guards will alert us to the oncoming assault before the attackers reach this area. It will give us plenty of time to prepare, and in their flight back down the path, they may trample some of the attackers, saving us the exercise of us having to fight them off. But to your question as to how we get them in the location we want, I'm still working on that. Now, do you have any further questions or suggestions on the placement and strategy?"

Gnaeus shook his head no.

"Fine, I will leave it up to you as to who is positioned where. Oh, one more thing. I want the campfire here in the encampment to be low, but the fire over by the tomb to be burning. It will deepen the shadows and allow our men to be better hidden. The attackers will only see the two posted at the tomb stone, which will give us further advantage when they attempt to attack. We will have the surprise on them. We'll discuss this more this evening before supper. Now it looks like you could do with some rest. Did you stand one of the watches last night?"

"Um, yes sir," Gnaeus admitted. "Two actually. I wasn't able to sleep."

"I see," said Gaius. "Get some rest now. I need my decanus rested and ready to lead his men. We'll talk later."

With that Gnaeus gathered the remains of his meal, stood, and wandered off to the pile of supplies. As Gnaeus walked away, Gaius leaned over to Matthias and quietly said, "Something he saw at that execution has gotten to him. For a soldier like Gnaeus Runius, who fought at the battle of Weser River against those barbarians, to be shaken over a simple execution . . . something had to have happened. I dare not press him about it. I could lose him, and we may need both the body and the mind. I'm going to look around again and check the paths."

Matthias started to get up and Gaius stopped him.

"It's ok; I need to do some thinking. Just stay here and relax. I'll be back shortly." Gaius strapped on his helmet and walked off toward the tomb.

Matthias sat there thinking about the previous discussion. He felt like he knew what had occurred at the execution, even though he had been in the infirmary for almost two days prior to the events leading up to and including the execution. The dream he had the night before kept coming back to him also. Even though it was now midmorning and the sun had started baking the rocks in the cemetery, Matthias felt cold and closed in. He stood up and cleaned up the area to give himself something to do and try to shake this awkward feeling.

As he finished the chores he had set for himself, Matthias overheard several of the men talking. Julius was trying to strike up a game of dice with Scipio and Lucius.

"Come on, there's nothing else to do. Let's have a nice friendly game to ease the time," urged Julius.

"What would we play for?" inquired Scipio. "It's another three days before I get paid. I suppose you have a few denarii to wager?"

"Well," started Julius, "I don't have any with me. I have to wait for payday also. How about you, Lucius, have anything to wager?"

"No," replied Lucius. "I had a small purse, but it disappeared when I became ill and went to the infirmary."

"That's not surprising," added Scipio. "Those attendants in the infirmary try to take anything and everything. My friend Antonius went to the infirmary after a slight disagreement concerning a couple skins of wine. When he left the infirmary, he was missing three weeks' pay. But the problem was he couldn't remember whether he had used the money for the wine skins or if he had it when he went in."

"Here," interrupted Julius. "We'll use stones as markers. Just a nice friendly game. Besides, we're on our own time."

"At least until it's your turn to stand post," offered Scipio.

Julius collected a number of pebbles and distributed them amongst the three. Next, he went over to the supplies and found a small wooden cup. Finally, he produced four dice from a small pouch from under his leather vest.

"All right let's get started," he announced. Julius handed the cup with the dice over to Scipio.

Scipio cupped one hand over the top of the cup and the other hand underneath. He shook the cup a couple of times and then quickly turned it over onto the stone surface. He removed the cup and took a look at the results.

"Curse the gods," he muttered. "Nothing. Here, see if you can come up with something."

He handed the cup with the dice to Lucius, who halfheartedly rolled the cup around in his hands and tipped the cup over to let the dice pour out. Two of the dice came to rest on the stone where they had landed, but the other two went skittering off.

"Easy there," said Julius, as he fumbled after the two rogue cubes. He tossed the two dice to Lucius. "Hold on, I have an idea."

He went over to supplies and retrieved a blanket. Julius dropped the blanket in between Lucius and Scipio in a rumpled pile. He then knelt down and arranged a well in the middle of the blanket. "There, this will cut down on any further escapes."

Lucius proceeded to rattle the dice in the cup and deposit them on to the blanket.

"Oh," exclaimed Julius. "Now there's a roll that will be tough to beat."

Lucius handed the cup to Julius who collected the dice from the blanket and back into the cup. Julius shook the cup with both hands and slapped it upside down onto the blanket.

When he pulled back the cup, it was Scipio who announced, "Well, I see the gods favor you just as much as they favor me."

"Yeah," started Julius as he passed the cup to Scipio. "I had the same luck yesterday. There I was winning everything in sight. And then one of the other guards went over to the base of the cross and brought back this robe. He said that its owner was no longer going to need it. He offered it against the winnings I had collected. I looked it over. It was a fine piece of clothing, so I said sure. So, I handed the guy the cup, and he threw a pair. That's all, a lousy pair. I knew the robe was mine. I started shaking the cup and tossed dice onto the robe. And guess what happened. Come on guess." The other two looked at each other and shrugged. "Nothing, absolutely nothing. I couldn't be beat until that roll. I lost it all. Everything. All the winnings and that godforsaken robe."

"So why didn't you try to win it back?" asked Scipio. He started to shake the dice for his turn.

"That's when it happened. It was midday, and the sky started to darken. Out of nowhere, the darkest clouds started to cover us from one horizon to the other. Then for a moment, there was not a sound."

Scipio stopped rattling the dice in the cup.

"It was the strangest thing, nothing. . . . Then a wind started blowing, lightning flashed, and it started to rain. And that wasn't all. Just as all of this started, the earth shook. For a moment, I thought the gods where going to wipe us off that hill. I grabbed my dice and tried to stand up. I remember looking around and seeing all of the onlookers heading for the city gates. Next thing I knew, orders were being given to break the prisoners' legs, so they would die. And we could leave. I grabbed a club and swung at one of the prisoners' legs. But with the wind blowing the rain in my face, I missed and hit the cross. When I hit that solid piece of wood the club was knocked from my hands. They are still sore. That's when another guard picked up the club and broke both his legs with one blow. By this time, the other prisoner on the far end had his legs broken. The one in the middle already looked dead. So the guy that won everything from me picked up a lance and thrust it into the prisoner's side. Sure enough, he was dead, no movement at all. But when he pulled the lance out all of this blood and water came pouring out. Like someone was pouring out a pitcher of wine. And then there were several flashes of lightning, and the earth shook again. When the order was given to leave for the city gates, they didn't have to tell me a second time. To be honest, we all sort of ran for the gates at the same time."

"So, what happened then?" inquired Lucius.

"Not much," responded Julius. "We waited out the storm. I have never seen such a storm. It would not have surprised all of us if the hill were to have been wiped clean of the equipment and even the dead we left there. Once the storm let up, we went back up the hill to retrieve the dead and clean up. Surprisingly, everything was just as we'd left it. Two of the bodies we removed and handed over to the local gravers. But the one that was stabbed with the lance, he was being held there until orders were to be delivered. But I didn't see that happen. Apparently, one of the other guards made a complaint to the captain who was overseeing things about how I stole his money when we were tossing the dice before everything happened. The captain decided to put me in jail until everything could be sorted out. And there I would have been if the centurion hadn't come along and pulled me out for this detail."

Matthias quietly moved away from where he was standing and walked over to the other side of the encampment. He mulled over the things he had heard. This started him thinking about the discussion between Pilate and Caiaphas. All of this seemed so familiar, but he couldn't figure out why.

About that time, Gaius returned. As he approached Matthias, he started looking over the encampment.

"Where are the other men?" Gaius inquired.

Matthias motioned back over his shoulder and started mimicking the collection, shaking, and throwing of dice.

"Ah, keeping themselves out of trouble with higher forms of entertainment," replied Gaius.

Matthias grinned and nodded.

"Well, I hope they enjoy themselves. I've directed Gnaeus to have the men clean up the camp, prepared the fires for tonight, make a list of needed supplies from the fortress, and prepare a couple of hiding places at the edge of either path in preparation for the morning. And here he comes now."

As Gnaeus passed, he acknowledged Gaius and Matthias with a nod and "sirs" as he moved on to where the other three were. Matthias heard Gnaeus bellow when he came upon the three—rolling dice. Faster than a thief on the run, the three men were up and busy at their assigned tasks.

Gnaeus returned to Gaius, "Sir, I have a short list of items we should have brought from the fortress."

"Very good, Decanus," returned Gaius. "What items do you suggest?"

"Sir, I would suggest another load of wood for the fires, a few more spears may be useful, and for some reason, we seem to be running a little short on wine," listed Gnaeus. "But we appear to have plenty of water," he added.

"Very well," said Gaius. "Select one of the men and send him as a runner back to the fortress, have him report the provisions to the captain of the guard at the gate, and then return. Make sure he clearly states that these supplies need to be brought with the evening meal. Please make sure the runner understands he is not to stop off anywhere between here and the fortress. Who do you propose to send?"

Gnaeus thought for a moment, "Lucius will be the runner. He's well-rested, and he's not likely to stray from the task . . . based on my judgment of the man."

"Fine," agreed Gaius. "Please see to it. I want him to get there in time for those items to be added to the evening supplies."

"Sir," Gnaeus stated as he saluted Gaius. After that he turned, went off in search of Lucius, and sent him off to the fortress.

Gaius turned to Matthias, "Have you seen anyone moving around out there?" motioning to the cemetery.

Matthias shook his head no.

"I wouldn't have expected you to, but I wanted to check. By the way, if you need to raise the alarm use the broad side of your sword and slap it against your chest plate. Even if you could whisper, I don't want you straining your throat. Not until we get you to a real doctor."

Mattias raised a hand to the wrapping on his neck. "Don't worry . . . I promise . . . it will be fine."

Matthias gave Gaius a half grin.

Matthias looked over Gaius's shoulder and saw someone emerging from the path where the temple guards had been the night before. Seeing the alarm in Matthias's eyes and his hand leaping to his sword hilt made Gaius spin around.

At about the same time, one of the two soldiers posted at the tomb called out, "Halt, go no further, or pay the penalty!"

Directly, Gnaeus appeared with sword drawn and confronted the individual. A moment later Gnaeus called to Gaius, "Sir, he's a messenger."

Gaius glanced at Mathias, "Come on, let's see what this is."

Matthias grabbed up his helmet and secured it in place as he followed Gaius. The messenger was noticeably nervous as the two approached. Gnaeus never took his eyes off of the man nor dropped the tip of his sword.

"What is the message?" demanded Gaius.

"Ah sir, ah . . . one of the Sanhedrin wishes to speak with you." The man motioned back down the path. "Would it be allowed for him to approach?"

"Yes, you may call for him from here," directed Gaius.

The man turned and called back down the path, "Master . . . Master, the centurion will speak with you."

Momentarily, three individuals could be seen moving up the path. The first appeared to be one of the Sanhedrin priests followed by two of the temple guards. As they got closer, Matthias could see the nervous expressions on the temple guards' faces. Matthias looked around and saw two of the Roman soldiers, who were preparing to go on post at the tomb, starting to walk their direction. He motioned to one and pointed to the other path and indicated that the other should watch the cemetery. Both men moved to the designated positions.

Gaius was surprised to see that the priest was none other than Caiaphas. "Centurion, do you know who I am?"

"Yes," replied Gaius. "I saw you when you requested this watch, with Pilate."

"Very good," Caiaphas continued. "As you'll remember, Pilate agreed to have the temple guard stand guard at the tomb with your men. Therefore, these two guards are here—"

Gaius cut Caiaphas short. "I believe Pilate agreed to allow your guards to watch from a distance, to be clear," stated Gaius. Gaius rested his hand on his sword hilt.

Caiaphas shifted slightly. "Well, let's not argue. I would like to have the temple guards . . . *watch* . . . from a point that they can see the tomb," pressed Caiaphas. "Pilate did agree that they may watch the guarding of the tomb."

"That's correct," conceded Gaius. "They may set up a small camp, no more than three guard, about twenty paces back down this path. They will have a direct view of the tomb entrance from the spot. That way they can run back . . . uh, report back on the status of the tomb. They may even be allowed a small campfire. I wouldn't want them to become cold from the night air."

Caiaphas turned and looked between the two guards back down the path. "I would prefer them to be closer to the tomb," Caiaphas said, just loud enough to be heard but not directly to Gaius. "But this will be acceptable."

"I'm glad this is agreeable with you," Gaius offered.

"The guards will return and set up their post before nightfall," continued Caiaphas. "I will leave one here . . ."

Gaius pointed to a spot down the path.

"And send several others . . ."

Gaius held up two fingers.

"Two more guards before dark. I knew I could prevail on your sensibility as a Roman soldier to allow our aid in this matter."

With that, Caiaphas turned and walked between the two guards back down the path. The messenger quickly followed the priest. The two guards glanced at each other as if they had realized they were standing alone, turned, and followed the messenger. At the spot where Gaius pointed out on the path Caiaphas stopped and addressed one of the guards, pointing down at the ground. After that, Caiaphas, the messenger, and the other guard proceeded on down the path. Once they disappeared, the remaining temple guard nervously looked back at Gaius, Matthias, and Gnaeus.

Gaius turned to Gnaeus, "Don't worry about these temple guards. Go on about your duties."

"But sir," started Gnaeus. "How did you know that the priest would ask to have his guards positioned right where you wanted them to be?"

"Ah, always accept good fortune and don't question it . . . for it may walk away," added Gaius.

"Yes sir," replied Gnaeus. "And sir, that was a very nice touch about allowing them to have a campfire. That added another barrier to an assault coming up from that path."

"Thank you for noticing," said Gaius. "Now, back to the tasks at hand."

"Yes sir," Gnaeus saluted and turned to finish the changing of the guards at the tomb.

# CHAPTER 9

As promised, later that afternoon, two more temple guards joined the solitary guard in the path. Prior to this, Lucius had returned from the fortress with a message from the captain of the guard.

"Sir," reported Lucius to Gaius. "The captain of the guard said he will see the wood and spears will be included in this evening's supplies. But the wine . . . he suggested that thirst would be better served with water, sir."

"Yes, that would be the prescribed method for thirst," replied Gaius. "Thank you, Lucius; report to Gnaeus to see if he has any further tasks."

Lucius started looking around.

"I believe he is over there."

"Yes sir. Thank you, sir," from Lucius, and he walked off in the indicated direction.

Shortly thereafter, the supplies from the fortress showed up. The fortress guard was good to his word. One mule was added just to carry firewood. Also, with the evening's meal were four spears and an additional wineskin. As soon as the porters left, the men not standing guard at the tomb started preparing the fires for the evening, and the spears were placed at strategic locations, if needed for defense. As dusk started to settle in, the fires were lit, and the meal from the fortress was unpacked.

"Roast chicken and fresh bread!" exclaimed one of the men.

Gnaeus spoke, "You have the centurion to thank. I believe he has made an impression on the fortress's kitchen."

"At least for the moment," added Gaius. "Let's enjoy the meal and then get some rest. We have to be up early. Gnaeus, have you explained the plans for tomorrow morning to the men?"

"Yes sir," responded Gnaeus. "Everyone has been assigned a position and knows what to watch for. They will be in place about an hour before daybreak as ordered."

"Good," said Gaius. "When is the next change at the post?"

Gnaeus looked up at the sky. It was clear, and the stars were just starting to show themselves. Gnaeus said, "Shortly, sir. About a half an hour. The moonrise will signal the next change. And sir, it will be a full moon. By morning, the moon will have set. As it sets it will be time to position ourselves."

"Very well," said Gnaeus.

A few minutes later, Scipio said, "Sir, do the legions eat like this when on a campaign?"

Gaius relayed the question, "I think Gnaeus could best answer that. Gnaeus?"

Gnaeus leaned over onto a rock he was sitting next to. "When we were campaigning against the pagan hordes in Germania, it was winter. Normally we would eat the standard rations, dried meat, porridge, and stews. But for two weeks our supply lines were cut by marauders. A legion needs food supplies every two to three days in order to feed everyone. After ten days, we were eating, or we were told we were eating, vegetable soup and anything that ventured too close to camp. We were even reduced to rating the horses from worst to best and started to eat them in that order. By the time supplies were arriving, a little over half had been eaten. They were trying to starve us out. Two days after our supplies arrived, the main battle occurred. After the battle, we found out they were running out of food. That's why they attacked."

Marcus jumped in, "I heard they had berserkers."

Antonius added, "What are berserkers?"

Gnaeus took in a deep breath and then continued, "Berserkers are men. Some say they are demons, but men just the same, that are so worked up that they act as though they have the strength of five to ten men. I've seen these men run into a group of twenty of the enemy, and within less than a minute, the berserker is the only one left standing. And you don't want to be standing next to someone who has been overtaken, because most of the time they do not distinguish between friend or foe. Those that live through the experience rarely remember anything that happened."

"What makes a man turn into a berserker?" questioned Marcus.

"Some heathen cultures use herbs and potions," Gnaeus added. "Others claim to use magic or some sort of mystical power. But most commonly, it's the bloodlust that takes hold of a man and drives him out of his mind to become a berserker."

Marcus started to ask another question, but Gnaeus held up a hand.

"Let me continue. When in a major battle and the lines between armies become mixed and blurred, one can feel as though you are lost in a sea of arms and legs, shields and swords, spears and arrows. It is very easy to lose track of which way you were going and which way you had come. At that point, some men can panic. I've seen some look like they've been turned to stone, frozen in place. Others will drop whatever they're holding, sword and shield, and start running. These individuals end up at the point of a spear or slashed with a sword. But a few become enraged, and these can become berserkers. And the more blood that is sprayed and slung from sword and spear, the greater the madness grows. Suddenly, the man seems to have the strength of many and shows no disregard for the number and size of the foe that surrounds them. Most start shrieking and screaming as they start to slash at anything within reach. I've even seen one man laughing like a hyena while charging into a picket line. And even though these so-called men, when possessed, are stabbed, slashed, and gouged, they fight on as nothing has happened. On an occasion or two, I have seen a hand or arm completely severed from a berserker, and they continue to fight as though it were only a scratch. And they do not stop until a well-placed sword, lance, or arrow finds a vital spot that no living creature can overlook, or they run out of someone to fight and are overcome with exhaustion as they start to calm down." At this point Gnaeus seemed as though he was slipping off into his memories. But he continued, "It's all the anger and hysteria that give the berserker his blind strength. But after, he has no more strength than a babe. . . . But he wasn't angry or hysterical. He was calm and sad."

"Who, Gnaeus? Who was calm and sad?" asked Lucius.

Gnaeus sat there for a moment as if he had not heard the question. But as Lucius was about to ask again Gnaeus started in, "The man on the cross. The one that some referred to as the king of the Jews. He had been whipped, not with a reed or a simple leather whip. They used a whip which had pieces of bone, metal, and stone tied to the ends of the leather strands. A soldier would be severely punished if he were to take such an implement like that to a horse or even a mule. The man had lost so much blood; he should not have been able to stand. And yet, they shoved a crown of thorns on his head and proceeded to hit him on the head with a reed. After this, they made him walk back to Pilate. Finally, they made him carry his wooden cross through the streets. Up and down the pathways, he dragged that cross. Only a berserker could show such strength, and yet, a berserker has to be wild with the bloodlust. There was none of this with this man. Only calm and even peace. Where his strength came from, I have no idea, but it was not that of mortal man. Even after they nailed him to the cross and stood it upright, he seemed to be in control of what was occurring. He asked his Father to *Forgive them for they do not know what they do*. Those that are crucified fight up to the end for that last breath of life before collapsing under their own weight and suffocating. Not this man, he waited until he was ready, then announced, *Father into your hands I place my spirit*. Then, he was dead. Life was not taken from him; he gave it up. That's when I heard a voice say, *Surely, this was the son of God*. I then realized it was myself that had spoken." Gnaeus sat there as well as the others, not knowing what to say.

"Gnaeus," Gaius spoke gently.

"Yes sir," Gnaeus replied as though emerging from a dream. "It's time for the change of the post. Come on, Lucius, you'll stand watch with me."

Lucius looked over at Gaius who motioned with his head that he should follow Gnaeus. So, Lucius got to his feet, collected his gear, and trotted off after Gnaeus toward the tomb.

Matthias, Gaius, Marcus, and Antonius sat there in silence contemplating what they had just heard. A few minutes later, Scipio and Julius joined the four by the camp's fire.

Scipio broke the silence. "What's going on? First, Gnaeus comes over to relieve us from the post and all but throws us from our positions, and then we come over here. And you're all sitting here like your best friend has just died."

As the two removed their armor, sat down, and started to eat, Marcus started to fill in Scipio and Julius on the meal's earlier discussion. When finished, Julius looked at Gaius and asked, "Is Gnaeus going to be all right?"

Gaius looked over toward the tomb and then back at the others. "Yes, I believe so. Gnaeus has seen much in his career, but what has occurred in the last several days is something different. Something that defies everything Gnaeus has understood. For some reason, the recent events will prove to have more effects than anticipated by Pilate and the Sanhedrin. And for some reason I cannot explain . . . I don't think this is over."

Scipio interjected, "You mean the attack on the tomb. The preparation we've been making for tomorrow."

"Yes and no," continued Gaius. "We need to be prepared for any type of attack on the tomb. That was the mission given to us by Pilate. And I do remind you that there will be a small delegation tomorrow after sunrise to finish the burial preparations of the body in the tomb. Once they arrive, let me know, and I'll handle things from there. But back to your question, Scipio, there was something different about this man. The way he talked, the things he said. He did not urge revolt and hatred like most of the rabble that Rome has had to squelch. No, this man was talking about love and peace. He even spoke against violence. That's why Pilate had such a difficult time in sentencing this man to death."

"But he was a Jew. Wasn't that enough?" asked Marcus.

"No," replied Gaius. "Whether the Jews or Herod or you or anyone likes it, Israel, and mainly Jerusalem, is part of Rome. And as being a part of the Roman protectorate, Roman laws must be followed. This man, this Jesus, had not broken any Roman laws. As a matter of fact, he upheld them, or at least as far as taxes went."

"What do you mean by upholding taxes?" asked Julius.

"Several years ago, Jesus was questioned by some Jews about paying taxes to Rome," replied Gaius. "You know what he did? He asked one of the men confronting him if they had a coin. Somewhat reluctantly, one of the men produced a denarii. Jesus took the coin, examined it, and handed it back to its owner. He then asked, *Who's picture is on the coin?* The coin's owner looked a little puzzled and then responded, *It's a picture of Caesar.* Then Jesus looked straight at the man and said, *Then the coin is Caesar's. So what is Caesar's give to Caesar, and what is God's give to God.* The men stood there bewildered and had no response. No, this man, Jesus, was not a threat to Rome. . . . It was the Sanhedrin that was afraid, no, I'll say terrified of Jesus. That's why we're here. Even Pilate pointed this out to Caiaphas when he went to Pilate to request our presence."

Antonius asked, "How do you know about this man and these things?"

Gaius looked over at Matthias and then back to the group, "Two years ago, I met Jesus."

Several of his men shifted in their positions. Glances were exchanged.

Gaius continued, "I was stationed in Capernaum. I had a servant who had been very loyal to me and helped protect my family. A good servant you can trust in these parts is difficult to find. One day, my servant became ill. He was paralyzed and was in great pain. I had a Roman physician look at him, but he refused to touch him when he found out he was *just a servant.* I then sought out a Greek physician to see if he could do any good. After an hour, all he could tell me was there was nothing he could do and that he did not expect my servant to live for more than a day at best. I was at a loss as to what to do. Then I remembered hearing some of the stories about Jesus. So, I started asking around about where he might be. Needless to say, I was met with suspicion and distrust. Finally, I talked with one of the more well-to-do Jewish merchants who was a friend, and I had done business a number of times and knew my servant. He agreed to take me to Jesus who just happened to be nearby. About an hour later, we came across a group of Jews, and my friend pointed out Jesus who was in the middle of this group having a discussion. As we approached, the group noticed our presence, and the discussion ceased. All in the group had a look of concern on their faces, except for him," motioning to the tomb.

"He stepped from the group and approached me. As he drew near, I introduced myself to Jesus and told him about my servant. I also told him of the diagnosis from the Greek physician. Without hesitation, he said, *I will come and heal him.* The gentle tone and confidence in his voice caught me by surprise. I was in awe of this man. I told him I was not worthy for him to come under the roof of my home. I told him all he had to do was to give his word and that my servant would be healed. I told him that I was a man under authority, and if I told a soldier to go there, he went. And if I told him to come here, he came, and if I told my servant to do something, he did it. Now it seemed like it was Jesus' turn to be surprised. At first, he stood there and stared at me; then he beckoned the others he had been speaking with to come over to where we were. To this day I will never forget what he said to the others. *Truly I tell you, I have not found so great a faith in all of Israel. And I tell you, many shall come from the east and west and shall sit down with Abraham, and Isaac, and Jacob in the kingdom of heaven. But the children of the kingdom shall be cast out into outer darkness, there shall be weeping and gnashing of teeth.* He then turned to me and said, *Go your way and what you believe it will be done for you.* I wasn't sure exactly what everything meant, but I had a confidence that my servant would be made well. Sure enough, by the time I and my merchant friend had returned to my home, we found the servant completely healed and still well to this day. I have told this story only to a few, because several have claimed it to be witchcraft. So, I have limited my discussion on the subject. But there seems to be more to this Jesus than what any of us know. And I'm not sure what others may attempt tomorrow. That's why we need to be up, ready, and in place tomorrow before dawn, in case any of the Jewish zealots decide to make a move on the tomb."

Gaius looked around the fire rim at his men. "Everyone understand what they need to do in the morning?" There were some uneasy glances, but they all nodded their heads that they knew and understood. "Very well. Everyone, get your rest. Morning will be here quick enough."

With that said, each man moved off to the spot where they had bedded down the night before. Matthias went back to his seated position against the rock, next to the fire. As he sat there, he examined the echoes of the discussion that night in his head. At the same time, he noticed he was staring at the guards at the tomb entrance, and their shadows on the tomb stone, cast from the watchfire. And as the watchfire began to lower in its intensity, so the shadows began to fade, as with Matthias's consciousness into sleep.

# CHAPTER 10

"Matthias . . . Matthias . . ." came a voice into the dreamless sleep. Matthias realized he was being gently shaken.

"Matthias," whispered Gaius. "It's time to get ready."

Matthias vision came into focus.

"I'll be back in a moment, get ready." With that, Gaius was off into the dark.

Matthias got to his feet and stretched trying to get his lower back muscles to respond after being in a sitting position most of the night. As he stretched and dressed, he noticed how dark it was with the campfire only being a bed of coals. But he could just make out the movements of several of the men. Two of them were fitting their armor in place as he was doing. He could barely make out the two posted guards from the dim watchfire. And there was movement over by the watchfire. Then he could start to see clearer as the watchfire began to grow brighter. Two of the men were adding more wood to the fire, which brightened the area in front of the tomb but created deep shadows around the entrances to the paths.

"Sir, may I assist?" said Lucius softly.

Matthias almost jumped, not knowing Lucius was standing next to him. Matthias nodded. Lucius helped maneuver the back and chest plates into place and started to secure the straps and pins until the armor was fitted. Lucius found Matthias's helmet and handed it to Matthias.

As Matthias pulled the helmet on and was tying the chin strap, Lucius asked, "Do you think they are coming?"

Matthias noticed Lucius was shaking slightly as Lucius handed Matthias his sword and scabbard. Matthias placed the scabbard with sword on his waist and looked back at Lucius, who still had a wanting expression on his face. Matthias placed a hand on Lucius's shoulder, looked him in the eyes, and gave Lucius the best look of confidence he could. Matthias then pointed at his own eyes and made a gesture to Lucius's assigned location.

Lucius understood. He came to attention. "Sir, I will be vigilant," Lucius said in a slightly louder voice.

Matthias now brought a finger to his lips.

"Yes sir, and quieter," whispered Lucius.

Matthias gave Lucius a grin, quietly slapped him on the arm, and motioned with his head to where Lucius was to be positioned. With that, Lucius was off without a sound.

Matthias surveyed the scene from the encampment. He realized he was still standing in full view of the watchfire. He noticed a shadow at the edge of the encampment to his left. He deftly moved into the shadow, making sure he had a clear view of the tomb entrance.

In the shadow, he found two of the spears leaning against the stone wall. Picking one he examined the tip and then checked the length of the shaft. It seemed to be well balanced. Matthias became aware how quiet it was. Not a sound. There was no movement in the air. All was dead still. As he placed the spear next to its twin, he heard something moving close by.

As he reached for his sword hilt, he heard Gaius whisper, "Hold." Gaius joined Matthias in the shadow.

"I wasn't sure where you were. This is a good vantage point," said Gaius as he studied the view of the tomb entrance. "The others are in their places. Gnaeus is one old stubborn war horse. He made it clear to me that he wanted to be one of the two posted at the tomb entrance. He said that there was no way he wanted to hide. If there's an attack, he wants to meet it head-on. He has Marcus with him on the post. Scipio and Lucius are over by the path leading to the fortress. Julius and Antonius are by the other path, out of sight."

Matthias reached over, picked up one of the spears, and acted like he was asleep.

"Oh, the temple guards, believe it or not, they are all asleep. But there's no way past them without stepping on them. I thought about skipping a stone down the path to wake them up. But I figure they would just get in the way. Let them sleep. Besides, it will be light soon." Gaius pointed over to a far hill past the city. "It's starting to brighten. Give me one of those spears."

Matthias handed Gaius the spear he was holding and then reached around and retrieved the other.

"I'm going to stand over in the hollow in that rock over there. I'll be able to see down the path better and watch your position in case they try to crawl over this stone you're standing by. Remember, don't move from here until I call, or if you see a position that needs to be fortified."

Matthias nodded.

Like a cat, Gaius was off to this position. From shadow to shadow, Gaius moved without making a sound. Once he reached his place, Matthias lost Gaius in the dark. Once again, Matthias started to survey the surroundings. The watchfire clearly illuminated Gnaeus and Marcus at the tomb entrance. He could even make out the location of the seal Gaius had placed on the great round stone blocking the opening. He glanced over toward the stone cemetery where the firelight flickered between the rock mounds. Again, the lack of sound was something not to be ignored. The cocks should be crowing. The sky was becoming lighter and the shadows less deep. No dogs barking. Everything so still.

Matthias looked up into the fading night, and there . . . a star . . . no, it was moving. It started cutting across the heavens, and then, it seemed to stand still. No, it was getting bigger and brighter. It was coming straight towards him. Matthias looked over to where Gaius was and wondered if he was seeing this. But before Matthias could figure out what to do, the object came streaking down, passed between Gnaeus and Marcus, and hit the tomb's massive stone. No, it stopped just before hitting the stone.

Both Gnaeus and Marcus started to turn toward the light, but before they were halfway around, they collapsed where they stood. Matthias started to run to their aid, but his legs seemed to lose the power of movement. And a weight pressed on him to where he fell back against one of the large stones, slid down, and ended up in a sitting position unable to move. He felt as though an immense chain held him to the stone and ground. He could not even move his head. He could only shift his eyes. Before him to his right, he could barely make out his comrades who lay on the ground, stricken in their hiding places by the path, now laying in full view. To his left were the others in the same position. Even Gaius lay not far away, looking as if he had fallen dead by the sword. But before Matthias was the light, still by the tomb stone. It seemed to grow even more intense. Even the watchfire, which had been blazing, seemed to have lost its power of illumination.

Then it struck him that there were no shadows. He had seen this before. . . . He knew this. . . . But how?

The light started to change. Within the glow, a form started to appear, and yet, the glow did not diminish. It looked to be a man but not a mortal one. The slender form radiated power that Matthias could not fathom.

This being glanced around, and then but touched the stone covering the tomb entrance with one hand. The stone rolled back to its earlier position two days ago. Where the dark mouth of the tomb was, now a growing, brilliant light emerged. It continued to grow in intensity to the point where the being outside of the tomb, with all of its light, seemed to fade. The being was still there, but as the firelight had faded with the being's illumination, now the being's light faded with that which radiated from the tomb.

Matthias wanted to shield his eyes but was unable to move his hands or close his eyelids. The best he could do was to shift his gaze to the far left, towards the stony cemetery. He noticed the cemetery had a glow about it. And then a mighty earthquake shook the ground. Several of the stone mounds in the graveyard started to fall apart. The sound of the shifting stone drew Matthias's attention from the tomb to the graveyard. Moreover, it seemed as though a few of their occupants were pushing through the earth and started to free themselves of their stony internment. They arose and stood next to their graves, staring in the direction of the light from the tomb opening. And then they turned and started walking towards the city's gates. A few were raising their hands by their sides, as if they were greeting a friend.

Matthias started to hear something, and it sounded like it was coming from the graveyard's former residents. It sounded like they were singing.

The light went out!

For a moment Matthias was blinded by the darkness. No, it was not dark. Morning light was streaming over the scene. It appeared the sun was just cresting the far hills. Now the tomb was dark again, and the being of light was nowhere to be seen. Matthias noticed movement by the path to the left. It was the temple guards. They staggered like awakening from a deep sleep. They quickly gained their senses as they surveyed the scene of fallen soldiers and the open tomb. One of the temple guards started to advance from the path's opening but was called back by the others. They quickly vanished back into the path.

# CHAPTER 11

As Matthias sat there, he realized he was not scared, just more confused. There was a feeling of peace and security. Then the immense weight of the invisible chains seemed to melt away. Matthias realized he could move once more. He still felt a little sapped of strength, but that too was returning as he staggered to his feet. As he braced himself against the boulder he sat against, he looked back at the scene surrounding the tomb. He began to wonder if the others were all right. But then he noticed they started to move as though waking from a deep sleep. He glanced back out at the stony cemetery. He didn't imagine it. Several of the graves were laid open, and their occupants were gone. He looked back to where Gaius lay and saw movement. Matthias carefully made his way over to Gaius. He bent down to help Gaius get to a sitting position.

"What happened?" Gaius worked to form the words. "I don't know what hit me. Wait, there was a light . . . it passed over to the tomb. Are Gnaeus and Marcus alright? I saw them fall."

Matthias looked over Gaius, toward the tomb. He saw Lucius stumbling over to where Gnaeus and Marcus lay. As Lucius reached the two prone bodies, they started shift and move. Matthias looked backed at Gaius who was trying to focus on Matthias's face. Matthias patted Gaius on the shoulder and nodded his head and gave a grin.

"Good," continued Gaius. "Help me to my feet. What of the others? And the tomb?"

Matthias helped Gaius into a shaky upright position. Slowly Matthias repositioned Gaius so he could view the scene.

"Oh no," almost whispering when he saw the tomb. "Did you see what happened?"

Mathias nodded again but without a grin on his face.

"Alright, tell me exactly what you saw."

Matthias opened his mouth, but again, a slight gurgle was all he could produce.

"No, not with words. Show me."

Matthias started giving hand gestures and pointing at different spots. As he did this, Gaius tried putting words to what Matthias was trying to convey. Several times Matthias had to stop Gaius because his interpretation was straying from Matthias's motions, especially when Matthias started pointing at the stony cemetery and tried to relate to what happened to the graves. As Matthias was finishing his story, the others started to return to the encampment where Gaius and Matthias stood. Some were able to come under their own power, but the two that were guarding the tomb were being helped by the others.

"Sir, I have to report that we failed to keep the tomb sealed," said Gnaeus, struggling to get the words out.

"Easy, Decanus," replied Gaius. "All of you listen. We were sent here to keep robbers from removing the body from that tomb. I'm not sure what happened . . . but I don't think Rome's best legion could have stood a chance to it."

A couple of the others broke in, "What was it? What happened? What will we do?"

"You are Roman soldiers, not a barbarian rabble," continued Gaius, trying to insert order. "Come to attention!" The men stood as erect as possible without falling over. "Decanus, you are to instruct the men in packing up the camp and collect the weapons. Notify me as soon as everything is prepared."

"Sir," Gnaeus saluted. Then as Gnaeus started dishing out orders to the others, Gaius motioned to Matthias to follow him.

The two moved off a short distance from the camp.

"Matthias, I not sure what has—" Gaius started, but Matthias cut him off by tapping his chest plate and pointing to the path leading from the fortress.

"I hear it. Someone is coming from the path," whispered Gaius. "Step back, we'll let them pass and see what they do."

Moments later, three figures appeared from the path. Each was carrying linens and either a small box or jar. Gaius started to move out into the opening to confront the figures, but Matthias held his arm in front of Gaius.

"What is it?" asked Gaius, so as to barely breathe the words.

Matthias pointed at his eyes and then motioned to the items the three were carrying.

Gaius starred for a second and then his posture relaxed. "They are women here to prepare the body. With everything that has happened, I forgot they were coming," said Gaius.

Just then the women saw the tomb and came to a complete stop. They exchanged looks and then starred back at the black opening of the tomb entrance. Then the women started to look around for the soldiers. Gaius and Matthias eased back behind some of the foliage but kept an eye on the three women. The women looked at each other and seemed to be talking to each other, but neither Gaius or Matthias could hear what was being said. It appeared the three had come to some type of agreement. They laid down the items they were carrying and then cautiously approached the tomb opening.

Just as they reached the opening, the first woman bent her head to enter the opening and froze. A voice could be heard from inside the tomb. Both Gaius and Matthias looked at each other in amazement, for they thought the tomb was empty.

The voice said, "Do not be afraid. I know you are looking for Jesus, who was crucified and placed in this tomb. He is not here; he has risen this third day. Come and look where he had lain. Now go quickly to his disciples. Tell them that he has risen as he said and that he will go before them and meet them in Galilee. There you shall see him. Tell them what I have said."

The three women slowly backed away from the stony entrance a few paces and then turned and started running back down the path they had come. They ran right past Gaius and Matthias not seeing them. As they ran past, Matthias noticed that they were laughing.

Just as they disappeared, Gaius grabbed Matthias's wrist. "Come on, I want to see who they were talking to," said Gaius as he started to rush the tomb opening.

As Gaius approached the tomb opening, he drew his sword. "Don't let him get past the opening, I want answers," Gaius said slightly louder.

Gaius hesitated for a split second and then launched himself into the tomb opening.

Matthias remained at the entrance with his hand on the hilt of his sheathed sword. There was enough daylight streaming into the tomb for Matthias to see Gaius, who appeared to be alone. Gaius spun around looking at every spot in the tomb. . . . No one was there. Matthias saw Gaius turn back to the stony niche where Jesus had been laid three days earlier. He stood there clutching his sword, but his arms just dangled at his side. Before Gaius were the sheet and burial wrappings that had been on the body, somewhat disarrayed but as though there should be a body. The only other thing in the niche was the head covering, which was neatly folded and laying where the head of the body would lay, if the body had been there.

Gaius emerged from the tomb. "You heard the voice too, didn't you?" questioned a confused Gaius.

Matthias nodded his head.

"No one is in there. When the women left, I didn't take my eyes off of the opening. No one could had left without me seeing. None of this makes any sense." Gaius sheathed his sword. "We need to get back to the fortress and make a report . . . I just don't know what I'm going to say."

"Sir," shouted Gnaeus, who was over at the campsite.

He was pointing to the path entrance where the temple guards had been camped. At the opening were two of the temple priests and behind them two temple guards. Gnaeus had summoned two of the other soldiers and was preparing to move to confront the four figures, but Gaius waived them off.

"It's alright," responded Gaius. "Finish packing the camp. We'll leave shortly."

As the two priests approached, the guards seem to hang back, looking a little nervous. Matthias had the feeling if he could say "boo" they would be gone in an instant. But they weren't afraid of the Romans. It was the tomb.

"Centurion," said one of the priests, "these two guards brought us news of what happened here this morning. Is it true?"

Gaius looked past the priests at the two temple guards and saw the disturbed state they were in. "That the body is no longer in the tomb? Yes. You may see for yourselves," Gaius motioned to the tomb opening.

The two priests had a look of almost horror on their faces. "It is a tomb, an unclean place," stated one of the priests.

"By our laws, we may not enter," added the other. Then the priest turned to the two temple guards and pointed to the tomb. Both guards shook their heads no and took a few steps back.

"You may take my word," said Gaius after seeing the guard's emotional state. "Nothing is in the tomb where the body was laid except for the burial wrappings. As for the details of what your guard has told you, I would guess it is pretty accurate based on their appearance and actions."

The two priests looked at each other, and the second nodded to the first. The first priest said, "We cannot have this story get out amongst the people. We need you to have your men only say that the dead man's disciples came and took the body while you slept. Here are two sacks of gold and silver for you to distribute amongst your men," holding up two large bags. "We're sure this is equal to several years' wages each of what a Roman soldier would normally be paid."

"There is not enough money to a Roman soldier to accept to say he was asleep while on post. It is an automatic death sentence," stated Gaius.

"We understand this situation," responded the other priest. "Caiaphas and a few others are going to talk to the governor to secure your protection. Will you honor our request?"

Gaius looked at Matthias, next over at the tomb, then over at the two frightened guards. "We'll take this up with Pilate. I understand the story you wish us to tell, but it will be Pilate's decision," said Gaius.

The priest nodded to the other priest, and he held up the two sacks. Gaius motioned to Matthias to take the sacks. As the two priests started to turn, the temple guards were already on their way back to the path entrance. The two priests hurried after their guard and disappeared down the path.

Gaius turned to Matthias, "Hang on to those sacks. I don't want the men to know what is happening until we talk with Pilate. When we get to the fortress, I'm sending all of the men to the infirmary. I don't want them saying anything to anyone. Depending on how Pilate wants to handle this, it may not turn out well for us. Come on, let's get out of this place."

The two walked back over to the camp just as the morning supplies were arriving.

"Sir," inquired Gnaeus, "the camp is packed, but the morning supplies have just arrived. What should we do? And sir," Gnaeus lowered his voice, "several of the men are becoming a little unsettled."

"I understand," said Gaius, "and I don't blame them much. We will go back to the fortress and eat the morning meal there. Have the porters take the supplies they are carrying and the camp items back to the fortress."

"Very good, sir," Gnaeus saluted.

"Decanus," added Gaius, "once you have given the porters their instructions, form up the men here to head back to the fortress. I have a few things to say to them before we leave."

"Sir," responded Gnaeus. He turned and went to speak to the porters.

Matthias looked inquiringly at Gaius.

"I'm not sure what I'm going to say to the men. But I don't want to lose control of them. Look at them. They've had a little time to think about what has happened here. And even though it doesn't make any sense, you can see the way they are looking around, they're becoming more nervous, and I don't want that to turn into panic."

Just then, Gnaeus returned with the men in tow. "Form up here," barked Gnaeus. "The Centurion has something to say."

The men lined up. Gaius looked into their faces, which showed an array of emotions. Some wore confusion, others fear, and a couple pure bewilderment. Even Gnaeus seemed to show a faint sign of uncertainty.

Gaius started, "This morning something happened that none of us can explain. There was no way to prepare for such an attack. Not even the fifth legion could have fared any better against such a . . ." Gaius tried to find the words to described what it was. "Thing. It is time for us to return to the fortress where I will make my report to Governor Pilate. When we arrive at the fortress, Gnaeus will lead you to the infirmary where you are to remain until I make my report. I do not want you to speak to anyone of what happened here. You may have seen a couple of the temple priests here a few moments ago. They are wanting us to tell a story to anyone who asks that the body was taken by the supporters of the dead man. When I see you in the infirmary, I will instruct you on what to say based on the directions of our governor. Moreover, remember this, you stood your ground and faced something that no Roman soldier has ever seen. You standing here is a testament to your resolve as a Roman soldier. Be proud. Show no fear. Decanus, lead the men to the fortress. The optio and I will follow."

Gnaeus turned toward the men and directed them into two lines. He then looked over to Gaius who motioned with a brief nod to continue. Gnaeus stepped off and the men followed. Gaius and Matthias fell in behind a few paces back.

"Do you think that did any good?" asked Gaius to Matthias.

Since Matthias's hands were full, carrying the two sacks of coins, he nodded and then made a stoic face.

"Maybe you're right," added Gaius. "They did seem a little more settled." They walked on. "Instead of leading the men back to the fortress, I wanted to follow to make sure no one decided to take off between here and there. I don't need for this to be any more complicated than it already is. When we reach the fortress, stay close to me. I want to see Pilate as quickly as possible. I want to get this thing sorted out as quickly as possible."

Matthias nodded again, showing he understood.

Just then a young wide-eyed boy came running down the path and skirted past the soldiers. As he passed Matthias, Gaius snatched hold of the boy's tunic.

"Hey, what's the hurry?" asked Gaius.

The child had a terrified look.

"It's old Ephraim," the boy stammered. "He's walking through the market! He's saying that Jesus has risen. The messiah is here!"

"Slow down. What are you talking about?" asked Gaius.

"Old Ephraim, old Ephraim," the boy kept repeating.

"Alright," continued Gaius, "what about old Ephraim?"

The boy hesitated, taking a breath, "He's dead! He died four days ago, but he's walking in the market right now. And he's alive." With that the boy bolted, pulling himself free from Gaius's grip.

Gaius looked at Matthias. Matthias pointed back toward the graveyard and motioned with his hands a mound and something rising up.

"You did tell me you saw bodies rising out of their graves earlier," commented Gaius. "Come on, we need to stay up with the men and make sure none of them stray." The two quickstepped after the column of soldiers.

# CHAPTER 12

When they reached the fortress, the gate was still closed. Gnaeus halted the men. Gaius and Matthias moved up to Gnaeus who was preparing to pound on the closed door with the hilt of his short sword.

Gaius stopped him. "Remember, take the men directly to the infirmary, and don't let any of them talk to anyone," instructed Gaius.

"Yes sir," replied Gnaeus.

"Very good . . . proceed. I'll deal with the gate guards," finished Gaius. And with that Gnaeus struck the gate door four times with the sword hilt. Movement could be heard on the far side of the gate.

"What business do you have?" came a stiff reply to the knocking.

Gnaeus started to reply, but Gaius put his hand on Gnaeus's shoulder.

"I'll handle this," Gaius said firmly. "Officer of the day," Gaius said in a clear voice. "Open the gate, it is full day and past the hour for the gate to be shuttered!"

"Who questions the keeping of the gate?" returned the even stiffer reply.

"It is Centurion Gaius and his contubernium returning from detail of the governor Pilate," stated Gaius.

A much greater disturbance was heard on the other side of the gate. Then with a creaking sound, the gate opened. Gaius motioned for Gnaeus and Matthias to wait where they stood. Gaius proceeded to walk through the gate, where he found three soldiers, all in different stages of putting on their armor.

Gaius barked, "Assemble yourselves here in front of me!" The three lined up in front Gaius with looks of dread on their faces. "Where is the captain of the guard?!"

One of the soldiers replied in a tone suggesting that the captain was not quite ready to present himself, "Sir, the captain is . . . uh . . . indisposed at the moment."

Gaius locked his eyes on the soldier and said, "Do you know where he is?"
The soldier nervously nodded.

"Well, get him!"

The soldier hesitated.

"Now!"

The soldier was off like a rabbit. He darted off to a small door in the adjacent wall and disappeared. A few moments later a man emerged rubbing his eyes. He had obviously been sleeping. After about four steps into the gate yard, the man looked at Gaius, trying to focus on the figure. The soldier emerged from the doorway carrying the man's armor. The soldier caught up with the man and whispered something to him that made him stop in his tracks.

"What centurion?" questioned the man. The soldier pointed toward Gaius while trying to maintain control of the armload of armor. Then the man came to attention. "I'm sorry, Centurion, we had no idea you were outside of the fortress this morning."

Gaius squared his shoulders and then released the fury of a seasoned Roman soldier, "Sorry? Sorry is not good enough! We are going to have a few words, but before this happens, I only address Roman soldiers, not women putting out their laundry. You and your so-called men have two minutes to properly dress and return in formation. Only then will we discuss the normal operations of the gate, the proper procedures of allowing access, a soldier's uniform, and other infractions I will determine while I await your return. Move!"

All four took off back to the small door. The captain of the guard almost ran over the soldier carrying his armor.

Gaius stepped back to the opening of the gate and motioned to Gnaeus to bring the men through. Matthias followed the last man and stopped by Gaius's side. Gaius watched as his men crossed the gate courtyard and into another doorway leading into the heart of the fortress.

"We'll make this short," Gaius said to Matthias. "When they get out here just stand there and look disgusted."

A moment later, the first of the four guards came stumbling out of the doorway trying to adjust the scabbard holding his short sword. He took a couple of steps halted and then turned, returning to the doorway from which he had just emerged. He reached inside and retrieved a spear. He then rushed over to where Gaius and Matthias were standing.

Gaius bellowed, "We're waiting!"

Two more guards appeared, one with another spear. They rushed to join the first, who was standing at attention. Before Gaius could say anything, the captain of the guard came rushing out to join his men. All four were now lined up in front of Gaius and Matthias.

"I have been discussing with my optio the condition of this guard," Gaius said with an emphasis on the word *condition*. "He is speechless with what he has witnessed here this morning. He had even suggested that if there were more of you here that your ranks should be decimated."

This last part struck a nerve with the four, who knew that one tenth of their rank would be executed.

"But I believe I have persuaded him to accept an alternate punishment. At the end of your watch, all four of you are to report to the fortress commander. You will list your transgressions to the commander and check them against the list I have prepared and will present to him shortly. He will hand out the punishment in accordance with the transgressions. Anything not reported to him which shows up on my list will have the punishment doubled."

"But, sir," stammered the captain of the guard. "How will know we have covered everything on your list? We have not seen your list of charges."

Gaius hesitated but a moment, "I suggest you be thorough. You have the remainder of your watch to contemplate your shortcomings. Now . . . *to your posts!*"

The four scurried off to their positions at the gate.

Gaius watched for a moment then turned to Matthias, "Come on, we have our business to attend to." As they approached the door leading into the fortress Gaius asked, "Do you want me to hold one of those sacks?"

Matthias nodded and offered one of the sacks to Gaius. He then extended his arm down and started shaking it to get the circulation flowing again. Then he shifted the remaining sack into that arm and repeated the process with the other arm.

Gaius hefted the sack he was now holding. "Sorry, I didn't realize how heavy these were. I'll carry this until we go before Pilate. Then I'll need to hand this back to you to hold until we turn them over."

Matthias nodded.

"By the way," added Gaius, "that was a nice scowl. I'm not sure how you were able to hold it without laughing."

Matthias gave Gaius a sheepish grin and shrugged.

## CHAPTER 12

"Let's get this over with." And they headed down the poorly lit corridor to the main room of the fortress where Pilate held his court.

# CHAPTER 13

As they approached the main room, voices could be heard. A visibly nervous attendant stood in the doorway of the outer room adjacent to the main room.

"Centurion Gaius," said the attendant. "The governor is expecting you. He wishes you to enter, but wait just inside the door until he has finished his business with the Sanhedrin."

Gaius turned to Matthias and handed the sack back to him, helping him adjust the two sacks in his arms.

"Will you be alright?" Gaius asked.

Matthias nodded.

"Right." Gaius motioned with his head for Matthias to follow. They entered the doorway and took about three paces before they stopped next to a set of columns which circled the main room. Matthias realized that standing here, they were in the shadows, not well seen by anyone in the middle of the main room.

There in the middle of the room were Pilate and the ever sour-faced general Atilius, standing behind a table. Before them were five of the Sanhedrin, including Caiaphas. The dialogue appeared to have started before they had arrived.

"You first tell me that the dead man's body has disappeared, and now want me to say that my soldiers were asleep at their posts!" wailed Pilate.

Caiaphas was the only one who seemed not to shrink back at Pilate's outburst.

Caiaphas spoke, "Your excellency, if the people believe that this man has truly risen as he prophesized, there will be no controlling them. They will fall away from our teachings and moreover defy the Roman authority you try to maintain."

Caiaphas waited a moment to let the last part sink in to Pilate's Roman demeanor. "This is a mutual benefit to both of our needs—yours to maintain the peace in the streets and ours keeping the people coming to the temple."

Pilate sat down in a chair, placed his elbows on the table, and cradled his head in his hands. Then he looked up at Atilius.

"I should have listened to my wife when she told me not to have anything to do with this man," bemoaned Pilate. Looking back at Caiaphas, "So you want me to spread the story that my guards were asleep while this dead man's followers rolled back the stone and stole the body. Do I understand this correctly?" Caiaphas nodded. "What did your temple guards see—they were there? You insisted on their presence."

Caiaphas looked back at the other priests and then back to Pilate, "It made no sense what they reported. They tend to lean heavily on the grape when not under strict supervision. It's not worth mentioning."

Pilate rubbed his hands, "So if, and I say if, I agree to this story how are you going to keep your guards from telling others what they saw? I don't need their story getting back to Rome, refuting any report I submit."

Caiaphas showed a faint smile, "The guards are on their way as we speak to Herod. Herod shares a common interest in keeping Jesus buried, so to speak. Herod is going to split the men up and send them to several different posts to guard the frontier along the desert perimeter."

Caiaphas motioned to the priests standing behind him. Two of them came forward carrying sacks even larger than those Matthias was holding. They placed the sacks on the table in front of Pilate and then returned to their former positions. Caiaphas held out his hand to the two sacks.

"This little token will hopefully ease any discomfort of the misfortune of losing a body." Caiaphas's smile broadened.

Pilate reached for one of the sacks and tried to pull it towards him. But he found it was heavier than he had anticipated. He partially rose from his seat and dragged the sack toward him and sat back down. Loosening the tie around the top of the sack he tipped the sack over. Gold and silver coins poured onto the table. Even Atilius showed a look of mild amazement.

Pilate straightened back up in the chair. "I will take this into consideration. Certain protocol needs to be followed and reports made. But my main concern is to maintain the peace. We don't want to draw Rome's attention any more than necessary. I'm sure you have duties to perform much in the same way I do. And I need to hear my centurion's report."

Caiaphas nodded and flashed a knowing grin. Then he turned and ushered the others of the Sanhedrin from the main room.

Pilate sat there for a moment staring at the contents of the overturned sack. The attendant who gave entrance to Gaius and Matthias approached Pilate from one side. He whispered something to Pilate that seemed to bring Pilate back from his thoughts.

"Yes, yes. Bring him in. I need to hear his report," Pilate instructed.

The attendant waved to Gaius and Matthias to approach the table from where they had been standing.

Gaius led the way to the opposite side of the table from Pilate. Matthias followed and stopped just off of Gaius's right side. The two stood at attention and waited for Pilate to speak.

"Centurion, I want to hear the full, true story of what happened. I don't want to hear any of the fabricated tale that these Jewish priests are pedaling. But first what is your optio carrying?" inquired Pilate.

Gaius glanced over at Matthias and then motioned to Matthias to place the sacks onto the table. Matthias obliged as Gaius explained, "This is payment from one of the priests to say that the dead man's followers came and stole the body."

"And what were you supposed to be doing while this theft occurred?" asked Pilate.

Gaius cleared his throat. "They wanted us to tell people that the men and I were asleep."

"Well," Pilate mused, "it appears Caiaphas's story to me seems to be consistent. Between what you have just deposited on this table and what Caiaphas left, there must be something pretty amazing he wants to hide. I want you to start with your departure from the fortress three days ago up to your return."

"Sir," started Gaius, "I'm not sure you'll find this report fully believable. I'm not sure I understand it myself."

Atilius started to step forward and say something, but Pilate held up a hand. "No matter how believable or not, I want to hear your full account. And after what has happened these last several days, I might just believe anything."

"Yes sir," started Gaius.

Gaius began by describing the collection of his men and moved on to their arrival at the tomb. He continued on describing the burial party and the sealing of the tomb. As he talked, Pilate stared off toward the far wall in the room. Yet he was listening to every word Gaius used to describe the events of the last three days. As Gaius continued, the late morning turned into midafternoon. As Gaius started describing that final morning and the preparations Gaius's men made for a possible attack, Pilate shifted forward in his chair and leaned on the table, intently staring at Gaius. When Gaius got to the part where the light appeared from the sky, he hesitated looking at Pilate and Atilius.

Pilate motion for him to continue.

Gaius swallowed and then continued. As he described being paralyzed and yet what was happening, Pilate stopped Gaius.

"Wait," said Pilate. "I thought you had fallen face-first and couldn't move. How did you see these things you just told us?"

Gaius hesitated a moment and then glanced over at Matthias.

"Sir," Gaius continued, "Matthias was the one who saw everything. He fell against a boulder into a sitting position facing the tomb. He too was paralyzed."

"Then let your optio tell his own story," insisted Pilate.

"I'm afraid he's not able to speak," add Gaius.

Just then Atilius leaned over and whispered something to Pilate.

"Yes, I remember the physician's report," mused Pilate. "Optio, come forward and remove the wrapping around your throat."

Matthias moved up to the table, glanced over to Gaius, and then removed the wrapping. Pilate stood up and leaned forward on the table inspecting Matthias neck.

"The physician stated you couldn't speak," stated Pilate. "Say something."

Matthias opened his mouth, but all that could be heard was a faint gurgling.

"Alright, that's enough. Rewrap your neck." Matthias started the process of putting on the wrap. "If he cannot speak how was he able to tell you what he saw?"

Gaius replied, "We have known each other since we were kids. Matthias can talk with his hands well enough that I can understand what he wants to say."

"I see," said Pilate. Turning his attention to Matthias, "So, are these accounts of this Centurion accurate?"

Matthias nodded.

Pilate turned back to Gaius, "Continue with your report."

Gaius cleared his throat and continued. Pilate slowly sank back into his chair as Gaius described how the stone was rolled away. Gaius continued up to the point where he and his men had approached the fortress gate.

Pilate sat there contemplating. "Optio," Pilate started, "Do you agree with the Centurion's account for the last three days?"

Matthias nodded that he agreed.

"Centurion, where are your men now?"

"I had the decanus take the men to the infirmary," replied Gaius. "I thought it best to keep them isolated until we had your decision on what we say happened this morning. They were also a little disturbed by the events earlier."

"Good, good," Pilate said as he pondered the situation. "Centurion, I want you and your optio to spend the night in the infirmary. Keep an eye on your men, maintain control. In the morning, I will send for you and give you further instructions. You and your optio are dismissed."

Both Gaius and Matthias came to attention, and then Gaius turned and left the main room with Matthias following. The attendant was waiting at the door with two other soldiers. As Gaius and Matthias passed into the hallway leading to the infirmary, Matthias noticed that the two soldiers were following them. He reached out and touched Gaius on the shoulder.

Gaius whispered without turning, "I know. Keep walking. Act as though they are not there."

As they approached the infirmary door, they saw two more soldiers posted at the door. Gaius acted as though it was common to have guards at the door. He walked between them and entered the infirmary, with Matthias following. Once inside, Matthias closed the door behind him.

"Sir," began Gnaeus in a hushed voice, "we have been relieved of our swords and our armor."

Gaius surveyed the infirmary. "It's alright, relax," responded Gaius. "The men look nervous . . . we don't want to add to their anxiety. Where is the physician?"

Gnaeus glanced over at Matthias and then back to Gaius. "He left shortly after we arrived. He wanted to know why we came to the infirmary. Before I could say anything two of the men broke down. One started laughing, and the other crying. The others just collapsed onto the beds. That's when the physician left the room with two of his attendants. Shortly after that several guards came and relieved us of our items."

"I see," mused Gaius. "Has anyone eaten since this morning?"

Gnaeus shook his head no.

"The two of you wait here," speaking to Gnaeus and Matthias. Gaius went to the door and stepped out of the infirmary.

Matthias could hear muffled talking, until he heard Gaius raise his voice. "Soldier, my men are tired and hungry. I think you better follow a centurion's wishes, go to the kitchen, and have a meal with plenty of wine delivered to the infirmary. If not, you may find yourself walking a post tonight, outside of the walls of this fortress."

Matthias heard someone hurrying away down the hall. Gaius came back into the room and shut the door. "I believe food and drink will be arriving shortly. Gnaeus, why don't you prepare some tables and seating for the food."

Gnaeus started to turn to follow Gaius's directions when Matthias moved to one end of one of the tables next to the wall and motioned to Gnaeus that he would help set things up. The two found two tables and enough benches and chairs to seat the eight of them.

Shortly thereafter, the infirmary door opened, and one of the guards stepped in.

"Sir," the guard addressed Gaius, "the food and wine you ordered are here. Also, sir, Governor Pilate wants to see you and your optio."

"Alright," responded Gaius. "Have the food brought in. The optio and I will report to Pilate directly."

"Yes sir," saluted the guard. The guard stepped back into the hall. Several attendants, laden with bread, meat, cheese, fruit, and vessels of wine entered. Gaius motioned to Gnaeus and Matthias to step over next to him.

In a low voice Gaius instructed Gnaeus, "You and the men go ahead and eat. The optio and I will be back shortly to join you. Save us a couple of seats. And Gnaeus, let the men have as much as they want to drink tonight. After what we've been through today, they deserve it."

Gnaeus nodded, turned, and started urging the men to the table. Gaius motioned to Matthias to follow. Gaius and Matthias stepped out of the infirmary into the hallway where the guard was waiting.

"Sir, please follow me," announced the guard.

As they walked, Matthias noticed that they were heading to a different part of the fortress. Finally, they came to a door, where the guard stood to one side and motioned for the two to go in. Matthias followed Gaius into the room.

This was not the grand main room but a much smaller room filled with jars, bundles, boxes, and stacks of blankets. Gaius and Matthias were led through a dimly lit path of stored items. Near the back of the room was a cleared area lit by a few oil lamps. A small, well-worn, wooden table had one of the oil lamps, a number of small pouches, and a scroll. Their guide led them to the table and then moved back off to one dimly lit area amongst the stores.

"Centurion," a voice emerged from the shadows. Pilate stepped into the light, followed by Atilius and three servants. Matthias could feel the hair on the back of his neck stand up. He was about to reach for his sword hilt when Pilate continued. "We have new instructions for you and your men . . . Atilius."

Atilius stepped forward, "Gaius, you, your optio, and your men are to break into four groups, each leaving by separate city gates in the morning. Each group is to travel in disguise as Roman merchants. You're to wear these clothes," motioning to the garments that the servants are holding. "You are all to report to the Roman fortress in Antioch. There you will receive further orders. As for the events of the last several days . . . they didn't happen. There was no tomb, no dead man, no . . . umm, unexplained happenings. You and your men are not to speak of these things that did not occur."

Waving his hand over to the table. "A modest sum will be provided to each man to make the trip to Antioch. Oh, and most important, since you'll be traveling in disguise, you'll need to leave your armor and weapons here. . . . They will be sent to you at Antioch."

Pilate shifted over to the table and retrieved the scroll. "These are your orders," added Pilate. "Deliver these to the garrison commander upon your arrival." He handed the sealed scroll to Gaius.

Gaius looked at the scroll and noticed the seal. "Sealed orders?"

"Yes," responded Pilate. "There are other matters included in that dispatch for the garrison commander. Please see that the commander receives the information. Any other questions, Centurion?"

"No sir," replied Gaius. "My men and I will leave in the morning as instructed."

"Fine, leave your armor and weapons here," said Atilius. "We'll pack your items with the rest. As soon as you're ready, return to your men. Eat and get some rest. The servants will bring the change of clothes with the morning meal."

With that said, Pilate cleared his throat, and Atilius returned to Pilate's side. Gaius and Matthias looked at each other and then started to remove their armor. Almost instantaneously, the servants started assisting, without a word being said. With assistance, the armor and weapons were removed within moments. The servants handled the task with surprising reverence. Finally, the guard who led them to this storage room motioned for Gaius and Matthias to follow. They walked back the way they had entered the storeroom. In the hallway, the two wordlessly followed their guide back to the infirmary.

Upon entering the infirmary, the scene was subdued. The table was in disarray. The apparent meal had been well supped. Most of the men had found a bed and were finishing off a flask of wine. A few appeared to be asleep. Gnaeus realized that Gaius and Matthias had returned. He stood up and approached the two.

"Sirs, your meals are over at this table," Gnaeus pointing off to one side. "There are two wine flasks also on the table. It seems that we have been given Liberian wine, a special honor."

"It would seem so," replied Gaius.

"Are there any orders for the men?" inquired Gnaeus.

"In the morning," answered Gaius. "For now, get some rest. We'll talk in the morning."

Gnaeus nodded and then sank back down onto a bench behind him. Matthias wondered if it was exhaustion, wine, or both that had finally caught up with Gnaeus.

"Let's get something to eat," said Gaius and moved over to the table. Matthias followed and sat down opposite of Gaius. As they ate, Matthias could tell that Gaius was bothered. At one point Matthias reached across the table and grabbed Gaius's wrist as he was reaching for a piece of bread.

Matthias mouthed, *What is it?*

Gaius hesitated and shook his head. Then with a whisper he released his thoughts. "This isn't right. We're being set up for something."

Matthias pointed his finger down at the table with a questioning look on his face.

"No. They won't do anything here in the fortress. Too many questions. If they want to silence us, they won't want to split us up. Too many chances for someone getting away."

Matthias tapped the table to get Gaius's attention. He mimicked rolling up a scroll.

"That might be it. The message in the sealed scroll could be to wait until we all arrive and then have us imprisoned . . . or killed."

Matthias pointed to two places on the table and then walked his fingers from the first point to the second.

"That doesn't make sense. They wouldn't be sure where we will be since they are having us split up and leave by different city gates. No, it's in Antioch where their plan will unfold." Gaius leaned back and rubbed his face with one hand. "I don't know if it's the wine or the day's events but I'm tired. You'd better turn in and get some rest. We'll have a lot of travelling to do over the next several days. I'm too tired to concentrate on what to do. We'll work on it tomorrow."

With that Gaius stood up, patted Matthias on the shoulder, and went over to an empty bed. He sat on the side of the bed for a moment then lay down and pulled a blanket over himself.

Matthias sat there for a minute taking in the surroundings and thinking about what Gaius had been saying. Finally, Matthias took Gaius's advice. He made his way to another empty bed. As he was about to lie down, he realized that this was the same bed he had awoken in three days ago. It seemed like a lifetime ago. But with that thought, Matthias laid down and sleep carried him away.

# CHAPTER 14

Matthew found himself in the dark. A cold, crushing dark. He felt his legs pinned and in one hand felt another human's hand. He was gripping this hand as tightly as the other was gripping back. With his free hand, he tried to explore his surroundings, but it too was held in place, cupped over his face. Was he buried? His mind was racing trying to put all of the pieces together. Then there started a shaking, which steadily became more violent.

Matthias woke up.

"Sir, wake up," urged Gnaeus.

Matthias started to jump up, but Gnaeus steadied Matthias in the sitting position on the edge of the bed.

"Easy, sir, you almost found this ledge in the wall with your head," Gnaeus rested his free hand on a stone protrusion where Matthias's head would have struck if Gnaeus had not averted the collision. "Sir, are you alright? You were thrashing around. I was afraid you were going to come to harm."

Matthias had put his hands out in front of him. He was looking at his hands and flexing them, trying to see if he was free and able to move. He looked up at Gnaeus and motioned that he was alright. Gnaeus held out a beefy, heavily scarred hand to help Matthias up. Matthias took the hand and found a vise-like grip. Gnaeus pulled him up and then again steadied Matthias, who was still a little wobbly. Matthias thought that this was not the hand in his dream. Yes, it was a very strong grip . . . and just then, he realized the sense of panic that was in the dream hand he had held. Matthias felt more stable. He reached up, patted Gnaeus on the shoulder, and gave Gnaeus a nod of his head.

"Very good, sir," responded Gnaeus. "The centurion needs you. Guards came a few moments ago wanting to talk to the centurion. He's out in the hallway and asked me to get you."

Matthias gave Gnaeus a sharp nod, turned, and headed to the door. Matthias opened the door and stepped into the hallway. Gaius and a guard were staring at him.

"This is my optio. I asked him to join us. Please continue," requested Gaius.

"Sir, as I was telling you," continued the guard, "Governor Pilate wants you and your men out of the city before the end of the morning watch . . . in a few hours. Food for the morning meal and provisions for your trip to Antioch will be here shortly. I need someone to come with me to collect the purses and scroll that the governor talked about last night."

Just then, several fortress servants laden with food came down the hallway. The three men moved a little further down the hallway to give clear passage to the infirmary.

Gaius stood there for a moment, then said, "Matthias, go with this guard and collect the items from Pilate. I'll return to the men and give them the instructions about traveling to Antioch. I'll also arrange who is traveling together and which gates they will leave from. There's not much time. We'll save you something to eat, and you'll need to change into the travel clothes." Gaius looked at the guard and gave him a nod.

The guard came to attention, grabbing the hilt of his short sword. "Optio, if you please," and the guard turned to lead the way down the hallway.

"Sir," the guard addressed Gaius, "I will take care of that other matter also."

The guard then continued on down the hallway. Matthias followed, but as he did, he looked over his shoulder and saw Gaius go back into the infirmary. Matthias thought that they were heading back to the same place where they saw Pilate last night.

As they walked the memory of the dream crept back into his mind. He started to feel the cold, trapped darkness even though he knew he was in the well-lit hallway. Just then, the guard stopped at a door.

"Optio, please enter, I have another task to perform. I will return shortly to escort you back to the infirmary." With that the guard continued on down the hallway.

Matthias entered the dimly lit storage room. He thought, *Yes, this is the same room from last night.* As he moved through the stacks of goods, he heard voices.

"Have the informants been given their instructions?" asked the first.

"Yes. Word will make it to the Jewish zealots as to the plans of the soldiers traveling as merchants," replied the second.

This made Matthias stop in his tracks.

The second asked, "But what if they make it through to the Antioch fortress?"

The first responded, "I've already sent a dispatch late yesterday to the garrison commander at Antioch. He is to watch for the soldiers, and if they arrive, hold them and await further instructions. Any survivors will be handled as deserters. The matter will be closed. The Sanhedrin can make their claims about yesterday's events, and the men will be listed as missing or killed by zealots, in which we will perform the necessary response with a few rebel executions. All will be recorded in the monthly dispatch as a normal report."

The second added, "We've also been receiving strange reports . . . uh, Jews are walking around saying that this Jesus has risen."

The first asked, "What's so strange about that? This is what the Sanhedrin was afraid of."

The second said, "Some of these people were reported walking dead several days earlier."

The first voice, "What else can happen? Make sure no one makes a formal report on these walking dead."

Matthias's blood ran cold. He quietly crept back to the storeroom door and slammed it. Then he shuffled back through the path and bumped into one of the stacks, causing a pile to topple, making more noise. As he emerged from the forest of goods, he was rubbing his eye and yawning. When he was in full view, he saw Pilate and Atilius standing by the small wooden table. Acting surprised, he came to attention.

Atilius barked, "Who are you? Where is the centurion?"

Pilate held up a hand across in front of Atilius. "This is Gaius's optio," Pilate observing Matthias. "Where is the centurion?"

Matthias pointed back over his shoulder.

"Ah, yes, your throat. Try saying something."

Matthias opened his mouth, but the same soft gurgling sound was the only thing he could produce.

"Yes, yes that's fine. You need to have that looked at when you get to Antioch," continued Pilate. "And where is the guard who was escorting you?"

Matthias again pointed back over his shoulder.

Just then the guard emerged from the opening in the stack of goods. He snapped to attention seeing Pilate and Atilius. "Where were you? You were to be escorting this man," glared Atilius.

"Sir, I brought the optio to this room, and then I went to carry out the centurion's orders," explained the guard.

"You!! . . ." started Pilate then he caught himself. "You need to stay with the optio whenever he is not in the infirmary. We are trying to control sensitive information. From now on, you will accompany anyone leaving the infirmary to their return." In a calmer voice, "Are we clear?"

The soldier stood as erect as possible. Matthias could see a single bead of sweat trickle down the side of the guard's face. The guard responded, "Yes sir . . . as you've instructed."

Pilate turned his attention back to Matthias. "Optio, take these purses and the scroll back to the centurion. The purses are to be distributed to the men for their travel to Antioch."

Matthias, being a little shaken by what he had heard, went to the table and started picking up the purses. After he retrieved five or six and cradled them in one arm, several shifted, and he dropped one and then another.

Atilius reached over to one side and grabbed a small basket. He dumped the contents onto the box it was sitting on and held the empty basket out to Matthias. "Here," offered Atilius, "make it easier on yourself."

Matthias hesitated, then took the basket with his free hand and dumped the purses he had in his other arm into the basket. He then quickly retrieved the other purses and the scroll from the table and placed them into the basket. Matthias picked up the basket and stood next to the guard. Both Matthias and the guard stood as statues.

"Well," Pilate motioned with his hand to the path through the goods, "time is short, and the journey is long. Move."

The guard grabbed the hilt of his sword. Matthias turned, headed down the path, and the guard followed.

It was a brisk walk back to the infirmary. Matthias wanted to run but restrained himself, not wanting to give any indication that he had overheard the initial discussion in the storeroom. His mind was racing. How was he going to explain to Gaius what was said? And the whole time, in the back of his mind, there was last night's dream. It was nagging at him, but he had to bury it for now and concentrate on the matters at hand.

As he entered the infirmary, he was surprised at the amount of activity. Several of the men were in the process of changing their clothes; others were wrapping up small bundles of food and placing them on another table. Next to the far wall, several of the servants who had brought the food were sitting on benches trying to stay out of the way. Gnaeus was near the center of the room, directing the bedlam as he too was changing cloths. Matthias went up to Gnaeus, who thought Mattias was offering the basket he was carrying.

"Sir," said Gnaeus, "thank you," taking the basket. "We'll handle this. The centurion," nodding his head to one side, "is waiting for you."

Gnaeus barked, "Lucius, take this and distribute the purses, one to each set of provisions. The scroll goes with the centurion's rations," as he handed the basket to Lucius.

Matthias moved over to Gaius, who was finishing dressing. "Good, you're back," began Gaius.

Matthias grabbed Gaius's arm. The expression on Matthias face spoke volumes.

"You've heard something."

Matthias nodded. In his hand he traced a "P" and an "A."

"Pilate and Atilius," said Gaius in a softer tone.

Matthias again nodded. Matthias motioned around the room to the men then raised his hand up to his throat and started to make a slashing motion, but Gaius grabbed his arm and stopped him.

"I understand. I don't want to panic the men. Just nod yes or no. Here at the fortress?"

Matthias shook his head no.

"In the city?"

Again, Matthias shook his head no.

"On the road to Antioch?"

This time Matthias nodded yes.

Gaius hesitated then asked, "And if we make it to Antioch?"

Matthias lowered his eyes and nodded yes again.

"The scroll, does it contain the instructions for our situation?"

Matthias shook his head no. Then he pointed to the floor and shook his head. Next, he made a motion to indicate the day before, and acted as though he had rolled up a scroll and was holding it.

"Ahh . . . Pilate has already sent the orders to Antioch."

Matthias nodded yes.

"Alright, we have some time. Get changed and something to eat. We are leaving shortly. Pilate is having us rushed out of the city. Now I know what his plan is. Go on, hurry."

Matthias went over to a pile of clothes that Gaius had pointed to and started changing. He reached over to the table with the food and grabbed a piece of bread and chewed on it as he changed. As he could he snatched pieces of cheese, meat, and fruit as he finished dressing. He saw Gaius move over to Gnaeus and say something.

Gnaeus nodded and then called out, "Men assemble in front of me, one line."

The men lined up in front of Gnaeus, and then Gnaeus went to the far right of the line and joined the ranks. Gaius stepped up in front of the men, and Matthias who was taking a swallow of wine to help wash down the meal set down the cup and moved to Gaius's left.

"Alright, you have your instructions. Each pairing will leave by their designated city gate. You have six days to arrive at Antioch. I don't need to tell you the danger there is if the locals find out that you are a Roman soldier with no protection. You are simple merchants. Blend in. Supplies are arranged for each of us on this table. There is food and a small amount of money for the trip. Most of all, not a word of what happened these past several days. Not here, not on the road, not in Antioch, not ever. Is this clear!" With their eyes looking forward they all gave a curt nod. "Good. Collect your supplies and prepare to leave."

The men went to the table and gathered their items and then lined back up. Matthias and Gaius then retrieved their parcels.

"Decanus, let the guard know we are ready," ordered Gaius.

Gnaeus went to the door, opened it, and stepped into the hallway. He then returned to the line of men in the infirmary. A hand motioned from the door opening to follow. The men filed out with Matthias and Gaius bringing up the rear.

In the hallway, Matthias saw that there were two guards in the front leading the procession and three in the back, one of which was the guard who had earlier escorted him to the storeroom. Matthias had not realized how much noise was made by a fully armed Roman soldier as compared to the dress of a common person.

As they reached one of the fortress's courtyards, the men were halted. The lead guards were conferring with the gate guards. The guard from earlier told the other two they could leave. After they left, the guard approached Gaius.

"Sir, I've done as you asked," the guard casting a wary eye at Matthias.

"It is alright. We're old friends," said Gaius.

The guard continued, "There is a sizable caravan leaving this morning from the east gate heading for Tyrus. It should meet up with another caravan going to Egypt this evening or tomorrow. One last thing." The guard slipped something to Gaius who concealed it in his traveling robe.

"Thank you, Marcus. Take care of yourself," said Gaius.

"May the gods give you safe passage," offered Marcus. With that he moved back to the entrance of the courtyard to stand guard.

About that time the guards opened the gate to the city.

Gnaeus called out, "Pair up and remember your instructions. Safe and profitable travels, you merchants of Rome." And with that the men proceeded into the city, each pair heading off for one of the city's four designated main gates.

As Matthias and Gaius walked into the city Gaius said, "Stay close, we have to hurry. The Tyrus caravan should be leaving. We'll talk more once we're out of the city."

They navigated their way through the streets, which were just starting to rouse from the previous night's slumber. As they approached the city's east gate, they saw the last of the Tyrus caravan passing through the gate. They reached the caravan and moved to position themselves near the middle of the procession.

# CHAPTER 15

The caravan was fairly large as far as caravans go. Matthias counted some fifteen camels, a dozen mules, four pairs of oxen pulling four wagons, six horsemen for protection against marauders, and at least thirty-five to forty servants and merchants on foot. For such a procession they were making fairly good time. After a couple of hours, with the city well behind them, Matthias moved a little closer to Gaius. He tried to find out who the guard was that told Gaius about the caravans and what he was given by the guard. But when he tried to get Gaius's attention Gaius waved him off.

"Not now," whispered Gaius. "One of the horsemen keeps eyeing us. We'll talk later."

About that time, that same horseman came riding up to the two. "Excuse me, good sirs. I did not see you when we passed out of the city gate this morning. May I ask your occupation and destination?" inquired the horseman from on top of his mount.

Gaius spoke up, "We, my brother and I, are spice merchants and were traveling to Tyrus. We understood that was the destination of this caravan," Gaius added.

"Yes indeed," replied the rider. "Tyrus is the destination. But I don't see any wares, no trade goods?"

Matthias thought the rider's speech and appearance sounded and looked Syrian.

"Ah, yes," replied Gaius. "We have been visiting family in Jerusalem. We'll collect our goods in Tyrus, and continue our business from there."

"Oh, very good," added the rider. "Well, I wish you good fortune and a prosperous venture." Then the rider leaned over and in a lower voice, "You may wish to not march like Roman soldiers. Your steps are in unison, and you hold yourselves too upright. You wouldn't want to give the wrong impression to the others."

Matthias looked at Gaius who was trying to conceal a surprised expression from the rider.

The rider continued, "I'm not sure what you are looking for, but there is no one following this caravan. You've been constantly looking back over your shoulders. Should we be expecting someone?"

Gaius addressed the rider, "No. We are just traveling. We expect no one. But we do appreciate your observations and insight."

"Very well," said the rider with a bit of a wily smile. "I would appreciate if there is anything I should know so there are no surprises on this trip."

"No," responded Gaius. "We too are also looking forward to an uneventful trip."

"Fine, fine," continued the rider. "You and the silent one may be interested in knowing that we have spotted another caravan. We will cross paths in a few hours. I expect we will camp together tonight."

"Thank you for the news," Gaius offered.

The rider straightened upright on his horse and in a normal voice, "We will be stopping for the evening in a few hours. Until then," and he rode off.

Gaius looked around to see if anyone had taken an interest in the conversation. Anyone close by seemed to be focused on their own thoughts or in conversation with another traveler.

"Well, so much for blending in," said Gaius to Matthias. "I'm still not sure who we can trust. I hope the rider will keep his observations to himself. It's good to know that the caravan to Egypt is near. Tomorrow, we'll be on our way to Egypt. That will give us time to think of our next moves."

Matthias took this opportunity to ask about the guard and what he had given Gaius. Matthias stood like the guard then pointed to Gaius's side where he had hidden the item.

Gaius looked confused. "What? Oh, the guard back at the fortress."

Matthias nodded.

"That was Marcus. He's my mother's sister's son. I looked after him when he first was assigned to the attachment posted in Jerusalem. I made a few arrangements so that he would be stationed in the fortress and not sent out into the city. He's the one who found out about the caravans and told me about this one and the Egyptian caravan we will be meeting soon."

Matthias traced a "P" and an "A" in his hand, then stood like the guard, next he pointed at his head and then at Gaius.

"Uh, you're wanting to know if Pilate and Atilius know that Marcus and I know each other?"

Again, Matthias nodded.

"I don't think so. When I made those arrangements, Pilate and Atilius had not arrived in Jerusalem to take his post. And I randomly picked two other new recruits for the same assignment to throw off any suspicion of favoritism. We've kept our association limited so that it would not be used against either of us at any time."

Matthias pointed at Gaius's side again where Gaius had hidden the item.

Gaius checked to make sure no one was taking an interest in their conversation. "It's a practice sword."

Matthias put a hand up to his throat.

"Yes, similar to the kind of weapon that inflicted your injury. If you would have been hit with a real sword, you and your head would not be here. I know it's only wooden, but it is better than nothing. Marcus was only able to get one of these practice swords since they are not counted and tracked like our real weapons. If anyone were to do an inventory of the practice gear, they would assume it had been damaged and discarded."

They walked on for a few more minutes, each contemplating Gaius's last statement. Then something caught Matthias's attention. Matthias grabbed Gaius's arm and pointed ahead and a little to the left.

"Yes, I think that's our next caravan, the one to Egypt. But it looks a little smaller than what I had hoped for. Nonetheless, that will be our method of disappearance. I hope the others fair as well. While you were meeting with Pilate this morning, I had a brief discussion with Gnaeus concerning my suspicions about going to Antioch. He had independently already come to the same conclusion. So, we altered the orders and told the men to leave the city in pairs and get lost, disappear. And that they were never to discuss what had happened with anyone. Since the men have not yet married and don't have families, this made the situation simpler. So now we must concentrate on our well-being. Tonight, we'll secure passage with the Egyptian caravan and get as far away from Antioch and Rome as possible."

They walked on a little further.

"One more thing," added Gaius, "we need to observe the others and adapt their mannerisms. Apparently, we are a little too Roman soldierish."

Matthias gave Gaius a big grin.

As they moved on, it was obvious that the two caravans were heading for the same location. It was an outcropping of rocks and vegetation. Matthias could see how a location like this would be well-defended and make it difficult for anyone to sneak up and attack the encampment. It would take a small army to risk such a venture. And Gaius was right about the Egyptian caravan; it was considerably smaller than the one they were currently traveling in.

As they got closer Matthias counted only two camels, five mules, two of which were carrying very little, only a single cart being pulled by an ox, and maybe a dozen men at best. He didn't see any horsemen. This last part of his observation made him feel a little unsettled. He wondered how safe the caravan would be to travel with. But at this point they didn't have much of a choice. Traveling to Tyrus was getting too close to Antioch and greater control of the Roman army.

The Egyptian caravan arrived at the encampment site moments before the larger caravan arrived. The two caravans arranged themselves next to each other with their goods and animals, side by side. They positioned their campfires in a ring to form a perimeter around their goods. Matthias and Gaius found a shaded spot near the edge of the two parties.

"You stay here and rest. Eat a little something, but do ration what you have. It may be a while before we reach a town to buy more provisions," Gaius said. Then he started to chuckle. "Provisions, doesn't that sound just like a soldier. Something else to work on."

Matthias motioned to the caravan, then to some of the bread he carried and the small purse.

Gaius nodded that he understood the question, "These caravans are mainly carrying their trade goods. They do not carry extra food. It would reduce the amount of goods they can carry. And they do not make their living on spare food. No, they will not part with a single morsel unless they know they will be within reach of a town or village that same day, regardless the amount of money." Gaius palmed the money purse they were given at the fortress. "This is a far cry from the sacks of money the temple priests gave us. I'm sure that Pilate's and Atilius's retirement coffers are a little fuller between what we brought and what Caiaphas had delivered. But this is what we'll have to work with for now. I'm going to see if I can find the leader of the Egyptian caravan and make the arrangements to travel with them. I'll be back."

Matthias sat back against a rock. He watched Gaius marching off in search of the Egyptian caravan leader. Matthias decided he need to let Gaius know that he was still acting like a soldier. He watched the others traverse the encampment. They tended to meander around a little. They also tended to acknowledge those they passed instead of focusing on a destination and ignoring everything in between.

As Matthias sat there, his mind started to wander back to the things he had heard earlier that morning in the storage room. He wondered if Pilate was wanting to get rid of the soldiers because he didn't want to explain things to Rome, whether he was trying to pacify the Sanhedrin, if he was just greedy and wanted all of the sacks of money for himself, or if there was something else. He was the one who ordered the man's death by crucifixion. And everything kept coming back to Pilate. It was like Pilate wanted the whole thing to go away. Even at the cost of eight Roman soldiers' lives.

Maybe it was a little of each. Matthias figured that only Pilate knew for sure what his motivations were. And then the thoughts of his dreams snuck into the back corner of his mind and worked their way to the forefront. It wasn't just the remembrance of the events but the sounds, the cold, the feeling of the unseen hand he was gripping, and even a taste in his mouth. But he just couldn't figure out how to describe the taste to himself, let alone anyone else. It all seemed so real. And it felt important, but he didn't have a clue as to what it meant. And he had no idea how he would describe something like this to Gaius without being able to talk. That was another thing. Would he ever be able to speak again? There had not been a lot of time to contemplate that. As he thought about not being able to speak, he started to worry.

As he sat thinking, Gaius returned. "You look deep in thought," remarked Gaius.

Matthias waved the remark away.

"Well with the help of the horseman, I was able to work a deal with the leader of the Egyptian caravan. We will be providing added security for the caravan. In two days, we'll be stopping in a small village for supplies. The caravan leader, a Mohmar Ahad, will give us a meager allocation of food for the trip. If we pool our travel funds we received earlier today, we can buy a mule to carry our provisions. When we reach our destination, we'll sell the mule, regain our funds, and move on to the next part of the plan."

Matthias looked at Gaius, gestured, and mouthed, *What plan?*

Gaius hesitated, "The one we'll figure out while we travel to Egypt."

Matthias sat there for a moment, scratched his head, shrugged, nodded, and gave Gaius a grin.

"Good," continued Gaius. "We'll make it. Regardless of what Pilate and Atilius had planned. They won't expect us to be going to Egypt. And the further we get away from this part of the Roman Empire the better." Gaius looked around and sat down next to Matthias. "I don't know about you, but I'm hungry."

Matthias nodded.

"Well, we just need to watch how much we eat for the next couple of days, and then we'll have more supplies. Oh, one more thing. The Egyptian caravan will be meeting up with another caravan out of Judea, in about a week. This is working out better than I had imagined."

Matthias started digging into his bundle and found some bread and cheese. Gaius noticed what Matthias was doing and started to search his bundle. The two sat there in silence eating their meal. At one point, one of the Tyrus porters walked by, acknowledged the two with a nod, and moved on. As they sat there, they watched the two caravans prepare for night. A few tents were pitched. The camels and mules were tied off on a set of ropes after their goods were unloaded and piled in the center of the camp for protection. A number of campfires were lit on the perimeter of the encampment.

As the activities died down, so did the sun. As the sun sank below the horizon, the sky folded one color after another. Blues, yellows, oranges, and purples shifted and faded as the greys sunk into black. A cool breeze chased after the setting sun. Matthias looked up and saw the thousands of points of lights glittering in the sky. He felt he could almost reach up and touch them.

Neither man had realized how tired they were. Between the long day's travel and the constant concern of what might happen the two sat there, content. And with that contentness came sleep.

# CHAPTER 16

Matthias awoke. Gaius was still sitting next to him, sound asleep. The greyness of morning was starting to brighten the day's sky. The campfires around the camp were dying embers. Matthias noticed the first signs of movement in the camp with the tending of the animals. As Matthias sat there, he realized this was the first time in several days he did not have that strange dream about being trapped in that cold, dark place. He searched his thoughts, trying to recall any hint of a dream. He had slept through the night, peacefully. As he was pondering this, he noticed that a young Egyptian, by the look of his dress, was heading straight toward him. Matthias nudged Gaius who stirred and then snapped awake.

"What is it?" Gaius urgently asked as he grabbed for the practice sword he had concealed in his cloak.

Matthias nodded his head in the direction of the approaching boy. Gaius shifted to a more upright position.

"Good sirs," started the boy. "Mohmar Ahad wishes your presence. He is wanting to leave as soon as the animals are prepared."

Gaius struggled to his feet, fighting the cramping muscles from sitting while asleep. He stretched and arranged his clothing.

Matthias followed suit.

"Lead on," offered Gaius.

The young man turned and headed off with Gaius and Matthias in tow. As they walked, Gaius whispered to Matthias, "I think Ahad knows we are soldiers. That's why he's allowing us to travel with the group."

Matthias nodded.

The lad led them to a simple lean-to that was being dismantled and packed. Overseeing the task was a short, bearded man who was dressed in desert-fashion attire.

"Ah, gentlemen," greeted Ahad. "I hoped you passed the night well."

"Yes, very well," replied Gaius. "Thank you for asking."

"And the silent one?" implied Ahad, motioning at Matthias.

"My friend is a man of few words," interjected Gaius. "He slept well also."

Matthias nodded, keeping his eyes fixed on Ahad.

"Yessss . . . few words, or perhaps none." Ahad shifted his focus from Matthias to Gaius. "We will be leaving shortly. I would like one of you at the lead of our company and the other protecting the rear. I will be at the rear of the procession where I can keep my eye on the goods we carry. I would prefer the silent one take the lead. I have been watching you since last night. You seem to be aware of your surroundings, constantly watching. You would serve well looking for any unwanted guests. And you," Ahad indicated Gaius, "I feel we may have a number of things to discuss. Is this agreeable, gentlemen?"

Matthias and Gaius looked at each other and half shrugged and nodded.

"Excellent," Ahad said as he rubbed his hands together. "The last of the mules are being loaded. I suggest you eat and prepare to travel. The boy will come and let you know when we are ready to leave. Gentlemen," Ahad flourished his hand and then turned back to supervising the packing, obviously dismissing Gaius and Matthias.

The two turned and made their way back to their night's resting spot. On their way back, Gaius hesitated at one of the dying watchfires. He reached into his cloak and pulled out the scroll that he received from Pilate. He dropped it into the waning flames. It smoldered but for a moment before bursting into flames. In no time, it was reduced to ashes, matching the rest of the embers.

"It's best that we don't have that with us," said Gaius. "I read it last night. It was a standard report. There was nothing in it about us."

They started walking again. Gaius pointed back over his shoulder toward Ahad's camping area.

"That went well," exclaimed Gaius.

Matthias looked at him with panic in his eyes.

"No, I don't think we're in trouble. Not at least more than what we're already in. I don't think Ahad would sell us out to the Roman command. He seems to be a wheeler-dealer. I think he may be willing to help us, provided we can help him. I'll see what his interests are and what arrangements we can make with him. We better get something to eat and fill our wineskins with water. There's a pool over by that rock."

Matthias pulled out his skin and drained what little liquid there was into his mouth. He held out his hand to Gaius.

"Are you sure? I can fill mine."

Matthias kept his hand out.

"Thanks," replied Gaius as he handed over his empty wineskin.

Matthias headed over to the pool with the skins. He kept wondering if Ahad would be willing to turn him and Gaius over to the Roman guard, for a price of course. Moreover, did Ahad really know who they were? If he did, how did he find out? These questions kept running through his head as he finished filling the skins. Just as he was finishing, the boy from earlier approached.

"Sir," announced the boy, "it is time to leave. Please come, come now."

Matthias followed the boy, who led him straight to Ahad and Gaius.

Matthias handed Gaius the skin containing water.

"Thank you," said Gaius. "The boy is going to walk with you at the head of the caravan. He knows the way. If you see any problems, send the boy back to us. I'll work the defense of the caravan depending on what the issue is. A couple of Ahad's men are armed and will join you to protect the caravan. You know what to do."

Matthias nodded but caught himself when he started to salute Gaius.

"There's a shelter we should reach well before nightfall. I'll see you then. Any questions?"

Matthias shook his head no.

"Good luck." And with that the boy headed off, followed by Matthias.

The caravan moved off with no fanfare. The only notice of the departure was the braying of one of the mules. At first, nothing was said by the boy or those who were directly behind the two escorts. The morning matured toward midday. Matthias kept scanning the horizon, which was simple since this area was fairly flat. Matthias would be able to give a warning long before any attack could occur. Eventually, Matthias realized they were moving toward hilly ground with large broken rocks. This started to concern him. He began thinking about possible ways the caravan could be attacked.

The boy noticed the change in Matthias's expression. "We will be crossing a stream that runs into the Jordan River," announced the boy. "It is not deep. The best place to cross within a half day's travel."

Matthias nodded.

This news made him more nervous. This would be a place for an ambush. Matthias kept moving in the intended direction, but he motioned to the boy to go to the back of the caravan. The boy took off like a gazelle. Matthias kept scanning the area they were approaching. Shortly, Gaius came running up to join him.

"What is it?" questioned Gaius.

Matthias pointed to the area they were approaching. He motioned with his hands the rough boulders.

Gaius stared back at their destination. "Ah, I see. It would make a good place for an ambush."

About that time the boy returned. Matthias pointed to the boy, moved his mouth, and then held up his wineskin that was filled with water.

"What did you tell him about water?" Gaius quizzed the boy.

"Just that we will be crossing a stream," responded the boy.

Gaius continued, "What else did you say?"

Matthias motioned straight ahead and nodded yes. Next, he pointed to the left and then the right and shook his head no.

"Is this the only place to cross?"

"Yes sir," the boy added. "But the next crossing is a half day's travel in that direction," pointing to the west. "The water is not deep, and this is the quickest way to go."

"I see," mused Gaius. Turning back to Matthias, "I think I understand what you're thinking. . . . Just before we cross the stream, I want you to hold up, so that the caravan can come together. We're a little too spread out, and it would be easy to hit and run at any point. I'll start working to move the rear of the caravan up. When you get to the stream don't cross until all of the caravan is present. I want you to first cross and check out the far side before the rest of the caravan crosses. Got it?"

Matthias nodded.

Gaius questioned the boy, "How deep is not too deep?"

The boy held his hand by his knee and then up to the middle of his chest. "Not too deep," he repeated.

"Alright," said Gaius. Saying to Matthias, "Follow the instructions. We'll get through." Gaius turned and headed back to the rear of the caravan.

The caravan pushed on, with Matthias studying all of the possible hiding locations where an attack could spring as they went. The terrain started to slope down as the rocks and boulders grew in size. The locations for hiding became too numerous to scrutinize. Matthias watched the young boy who was leading the caravan. He acted as though he could be walking through a local market. No sign of tension or worry.

Matthias started to think that he was worrying over something that didn't exist. They did join that first caravan at the last minute as it left Jerusalem. And then they changed to another caravan, going in a different direction. Just as he was completing this thought, they came upon the stream they had to cross. The boy was about to start wading across, and Matthias stopped him. He motioned to the young lad to stay put where he was. Matthias glanced back seeing the caravan starting to bunch up behind them. Then Gaius came forward.

"We don't need to loiter here for long," said Gaius uneasily. "There are plenty of hiding places. Take the boy and go on across. The rest of the caravan will wait until you cross and check out the other side. Signal me when you feel it is safe for the rest of the caravan."

Matthias nodded, patted the boy on the shoulder, and pointed across to the other side. One could easily throw a stone to the other side. As they started to wade across, Matthias felt the welcoming coolness of the water compared to the local heat. The water was not flowing swiftly, but there was a noticeable current. In the middle of the stream, the water reached to Matthias's waist, about chest high on the young lad.

Matthias started focusing on the far shore and its surroundings. A number of bushes and large boulders populated the shore. A path led past a clump of bushes to the left. The boy was first to reach the stream edge, closely followed by Matthias. The boy started moving to the path, but Matthias reached out and grabbed his shoulder. Matthias scanned the surroundings.

The boy looked at Matthias and then also surveyed the area. "Sir," said the boy, "I'm not sure what you are looking for, but nothing is here."

Matthias patted the boy on his shoulder and gestured for the boy to stay where he was. Matthias walked back to the edge of the stream and motioned for the caravan to come across. He could see Gaius urging the caravan to start crossing. The caravan moved through the stream without any real issues. Matthias could see Ahad and Gaius just starting to wade in when he saw two men materialize from behind small boulders on either side of Gaius. But Gaius must have heard something, because he was ready.

He brandished the practice sword while dodging the first attacker and applied a blow to the back of the man's neck. The first attacker dropped at the edge of the water and lay motionless. The other attacker was more hesitant about blindly lunging at Gaius. Then two more men came from behind a set of bushes, closing in on Gaius.

Matthias tried to yell, but there was no sound. The caravan splashed their way across the stream. It was almost across the stream when Matthias started back into the stream to assist Gaius.

Suddenly hearing from behind the boy yelling out, "Sir, look out . . . behind you."

As Matthias turned to see what the boy was yelling about, another attacker jumped at Matthias, hitting Matthias in the chest, and knocking him backwards into the stream. Even though it was not even hip deep, Matthias was totally submerged. He kept trying to reach for something, anything to pull himself up. He hit the bottom and instinctively tried to sit up. Just as his face started to break the surface, his attacker grabbed his tunic at the shoulders and lifted him part way out of the water.

Matthias sputtered and tried to get a gulp of air. At the same time, he tried to get his feet back under himself, so he could stand or at least kneel. But his assailant had another idea. Before Matthias could gain his footing or fully fill his lungs, he was thrust back under water. He was laying on his back starring up at the sky and his foe. It was hard to see him clearly. The flowing water distorted his view. But the man was burly with a mass of hair on his head and face.

Matthias tried to reach up and grab the man. There was nothing in his reach except the two strong arms holding him under. He had nothing to push off from. Matthias thrashed but was not accomplishing anything. His lungs were burning. He felt his chest starting to heave to expel the stale air. Matthias saw something dangling from the man's neck. He made one last attempt and grabbed the dangling item. It fit in the palm of his hand. Matthias pulled with everything he had left. He noticed that the man's face was getting closer to the water's surface. And then the cord holding the item broke.

At that moment, the sides of Matthias's vision started to blur and darken to form a tunnel. As the tunnel narrowed, closing in on his vision, he could feel his strength fade away. The tunnel closed into total blackness.

# CHAPTER 17

It was bright. Matthew open his eyes, but everything was blurry, hazy, and bright.

"Doctor, he's awake," called a voice.

There was a shape hovering next to him. It was joined by a second fuzzy form.

"Father Mathew," said a new voice. "Please, lie still. You are safe."

Matthew's sight was starting to clear, but he was squinting due to the brightness. Matthew raised a hand to his eyes and then moved his hand down to his throat. Nothing there. "Where am I?"

"You are in the mine hospital," said the voice. "Do you remember what happened?"

The image was becoming sharper. "Doctor Tanner?" asked Matthew.

"Yes," replied the doctor. "You've been through a lot. What is the last thing you remember?"

"I was being held under water by this man," answered Matthew.

The doctor looked over at the other person. Matthew realized it was Mrs. Johnston, the hospital nurse. "Mrs. Johnston, I think you need to let them know he's awake," suggested the doctor.

"Yes sir," acknowledged Mrs. Johnston. "There are the others out in the waiting room. Should I tell them?"

"Yes, but tell them to make it short," added the doctor.

Mrs. Johnston moved out of Matthew's vision. As he tried to see where she went, he noticed a small vase sitting on a short table besides his bed. In the vase were five daisy-like flowers.

The doctor noticed that he was staring at the flowers. "Robin's plantain, first flowers out this spring," commented the doctor. "Little Rachel brought those for you. She and the other children at the orphanage have

158

been asking for you, but I think you need to rest a couple of days first. Matthew, there are a few things we need to discuss."

"Alright," said Matthew. He started to feel drowsy.

"I've given you a sedative," continued the doctor. "Most of your injuries were minor. Your right hand was lacerated. A few stitches and it will be good as new."

Matthew raised his right hand. He hadn't even noticed the bandaged limb. As the doctor continued, Matthew tried flexing his fingers. They were stiff and a little painful. He laid his arm back down and tried focusing on the doctor as he was starting to drift back to sleep.

"We'll talk more about your other injury when you wake up." Matthew barely heard the last couple of words.

Matthew heard a soft sound next to him. "Father Matthew," it was Mrs. Johnston. Matthew slowly opened his eyes. "Good morning. I have a little breakfast here, but I'll give you a few minutes to wake up."

Matthew could smell eggs and bread. He was starting to feel hungry. "What day is it? How long was I asleep?"

"Well, today is Thursday, April twelfth," replied Mrs. Johnston. "As far as asleep, you slept through the night. But before that, you were unconscious for two days, since they brought you out of the mine."

"How long was I in the mine?" asked Matthew.

Mrs. Johnston thought for a moment, "I believe it was a little over a day. Are you feeling hungry? Do you feel like eating a little something?"

"Yes, please," as Matthew tried to sit up. He made it part way, hesitated, then sunk back down.

"Here let me help you." Mrs. Johnston helped raise Matthew to a sitting position and placed pillows behind him.

"Thank you. I seem to be a little weak and sore," said Matthew as he rested back into the pillows.

"With all you've been through, I'm not surprised," as Mrs. Johnston moved the tray of food to Matthew's lap. "When you finish, Doctor Tanner wants to talk with you. I'll be back shortly to check on you." With that, she left to perform her other duties.

Matthew started to eat the meal. After a few bites he started to realize how hungry he was. And shouldn't he be hungry? He had last eaten over four days ago. Before he knew it, he was finishing off the eggs and oatmeal. He was starting on the last piece of bread with a bit of strawberry preserve when it hit him. He was thinking about the bread and how it was so much different from that of the fortress. A flood of memories washed over him.

"How are you feeling today?" asked Doctor Tanner.

Matthew hesitated a moment, sorting out his thoughts.

"Matthew?"

"Yes, doctor," Matthew responded. "I'm sorry, my thoughts were elsewhere."

"I was asking how you were feeling today," continued the doctor.

"I'm a little weak and sore, but other than that, I think you'll need to tell me," replied Matthew.

The doctor pulled up a chair and sat next to Matthew's bed. "All in all, you're in surprisingly good shape. The hand is minor and should be better in a week or two. There are a few stitches I'll need to remove later next week." The doctor hesitated.

"Yes, doctor?" Matthew could see there was something bothering the doctor.

"It's your left foot. I tried to do what I could, but I'm afraid it won't totally heal where you can walk on it normally."

Matthew started to reach down to his left leg.

"It's still there. I was able to maintain the blood flow, but the bones were crushed in the ankle. I've immobilized your foot to allow it to heal. You will probably have a limp for the rest of your life."

Matthew tried moving his foot. It wouldn't move. Next, he tried to wiggle his toes. That he could do and felt the movement.

The doctor added, "The doctors at one of the larger hospitals might be able to do something for you, but it will require surgery. Possibly several surgeries."

Matthew rubbed the upper part of his left leg. "Thank you, doctor. I know you have done everything possible."

"Matthew, yesterday I asked you what was the last thing you remembered. Do you remember?" Matthew nodded. "So, what was the last thing you remembered?"

"In the mine?" asked Matthew.

"Yes," inquired the doctor.

"I was pinned by my foot, and the ceiling was falling down. I covered my face with my hand," raising his bandaged limb. "I was holding Ben's hand, in my left hand! Did you find them . . . are they ok?"

"Yes, yes. You need to stay calm. I don't want you to do any more dam-age to that foot," urged the doctor. "One other question, yesterday I asked you what was the last thing you remembered. And I just asked you the same thing, but you gave me two different answers. Why did you say you were being held under water?"

Matthew thought about it for a second. "I was a little confused, just waking up."

"Excuse me, doctor," said a voice from the other side of a screen next to Matthew's bed.

Matthew knew that voice. "Jack!"

Jack poked his head around. "Can a hero have a visitor or two?"

The doctor stood up. "I think a few minutes would not hurt." Turning back to Matthew, "But I want you to stay quiet. No moving around."

Matthew gave the doctor a nod. The doctor moved past Jack, giving him a look as if to say, *Keep it short.* Jack took the doctor's chair.

"You're looking a lot better now than when we found you," said Jack. "How are you feeling?"

"A little weak and sore," replied Matthew, "but happy to be out of the mine. What happened? I was beginning to think there was no way out."

"It appears there were a number of small earthquakes that hit the mines. It's not impossible, but very, very rare for this area. That block from the ceiling that fell between us took several hours to break up and remove. Thankfully, a number of the men had left the union meeting early and ar-rived to help with the search. When we got to you, you were pretty much covered in small rubble. We quickly realized your leg was pinned and were able to shift that boulder. But your hand . . ." Jack looked a little sheep-ish. "We still could not free you. I was starting to think we would have to amputate your arm. Once we cleared the rubble from around your arm and hand, we were shocked to find you had a death grip on someone else's hand. After prying your and his hands apart, we were able to dig further to free the others. If you had not hung on to Ben, we would have not found them. You saved them."

"I think you're the one who is confused," countered Matthew. "You and your team are the ones who saved the four of us."

"We were just doing our job," replied Jack. "But there is one thing that was confusing. When we found you, you were soaking wet. Your clothing was dripping, but the rubble around you was dry. I've never seen anything like it."

Matthew just shrugged. Right then, the two could hear whispering from the other side of the screen.

"Oh yes, there are a few others that want to see you. Gentlemen." Ben, Seth, and Samuel came from behind the screen and arrayed themselves at the foot of Matthew's bed. Seth and Samuel had been wearing ball caps which they had removed and wadded up in their hands, in the middle of their chests.

"Father," started Ben. "We want to thank you for staying with us."

Matthew started to raise his left hand.

"Please, Father, you could have let go and pulled your hand back to protect yourself, but you didn't. You stayed with us, giving us hope." The other two nodded in agreement. "And Father Matthew, you have the strongest grip I have ever experienced. But I knew as long as you hung onto my hand, we would be all right. You were the light in our darkness." Ben was beginning to get a little choked up.

Jack noticed that Matthew was at a loss of words.

"Alright, men, your shift is going to begin soon," Jack directed. "And Father Matthew is needing his rest."

"Yes sir," replied Ben. "Come on, lads, we have our work. Father, if there's anything you need, just say the word."

"Thank you," Matthew humbly responded. "God go with you and protect you." With that the three disappeared back behind the screen. With the sound of their leaving, Matthew asked, "They're not going back down now, after what they've been through?"

Jack shook his head. "No, not for another couple of days. They are doing above-ground maintenance. Then they'll start with shallow mine work where the coal exits to the coal train yard. After that, it will be up to them whether they return to the regular mine work or find something else to do." Jack stood up and glanced around the screen. "I've been watching them the last couple of days. Ben will be all right. He knows the drill. But the other two, I'm not sure. They were pretty shook-up. They have been following Ben everywhere he goes. The two used to talk so much it was hard to get them to be quiet. Now, I don't think I've heard six words out of either of them. Which, I need to be going to keep an eye on them. Get better. I'll check in later." With that Jack too disappeared around the screen before Matthew could say a word.

Matthew sat there contemplating a question. *Could he go back down into the depths of the mine?* Now he had an appreciation for what Pappy had told him on the way back from the train station concerning his experience in the mine. Matthew got a cold shiver down his back thinking about this. He also had a new admiration for these men that daily risked their lives digging through the depths of the Earth.

"Father, how are we doing?" asked Mrs. Johnston. She came around the screen with a small tray. She set it down on the bedside table.

"I'm doing fine. It's been an interesting morning so far. By chance has the doctor said when I can get up and move around?"

"Oh, I expect it will be a few days before he'll want you putting any weight on that foot," she said as she produced a thermometer. "Place this under your tongue." She took Matthew's wrist and looked at her watch. "I'll talk to the doctor and see if perhaps tomorrow we can get you into a wheelchair and take you for a stroll outside."

She put his arm back down and removed the thermometer from his mouth, holding it up and rotating it to read the temperature. "I understand that tomorrow will be a beautiful spring day. Well, temperature is normal, and your heartrate is steady and strong." She reached over, picked up a clipboard, and wrote down the information. "Do you feel up to a few more visitors?"

Matthew said, "Sure." He tried to sit up a little straighter.

"Here, let me help." Mrs. Johnston set down the clipboard and started adjusting the pillows behind Matthew. "There . . . better?"

Matthew nodded. "I'm not used to not being able to do this myself."

"Well, don't think I'll be waiting on you hand and foot," continued Mrs. Johnston. "You'll be needing every bit of your strength when we start getting you on your feet. A few more days of rest won't hurt you. But for now, you'll stay put and rest. Now, ready for your visitors?"

"Yes, ma'am," Matthew said with a sheepish grin.

Mrs. Johnston picked up the tray and headed back around the screen. "Gentlemen, I'm finished. Father Matthew can see you now."

Matthew was trying to figure out who Mrs. Johnston was talking too.

Father Griffith and Bishop Mayweather cautiously rounded the end of the screen. Matthew was dumbfounded.

"Father, we are most happy to see you," announced Bishop Mayweather.

"Matthew, we feared the worst when we heard the news of the cave-in," added Father Griffith. "As soon as we heard we tried to get tickets to return."

"He even tried to get us on the coal train, but they shut the tracks down because the bridge trestles had to be checked before the trains could pass," said the bishop.

"The doctor told us that you are in surprisingly good shape for what you've been through," continued Father Griffith. "But your foot . . . is there much pain?"

Matthew had a broad smile. "Not much, but the doctor has been keeping me comfortable."

"Father, we understand you are a hero," said Mayweather. "You saved three men."

Matthew looked almost ashamed.

"Matthew, why were you down in the mine?" asked Father Griffith.

Matthew looked up. "I was needed. There were not enough men to start the search. They always go down in pairs."

The bishop looked at Griffith, who nodded his head in agreement with Matthew's statement.

"Gentlemen," Mrs. Johnston had returned. "I thought you might want another chair. Please make yourselves comfortable. Matthew, if the pain becomes uncomfortable or you need something, let me know. I won't be far away." She gave the other two a look, letting them know to be on good behavior.

"Thank you, Mrs. Johnston, I'm fine," replied Matthew.

She cleared her throat and left.

Father Griffith sat in the chair closest to Matthew. The bishop took the other chair that Mrs. Johnston had brought.

"Matthew, we're not mad at you, just very concerned," said Father Griffith. "And in what little time we've been here, we have heard some strange things."

"What do you mean?" Matthew asked.

The father and the bishop looked at each other before Father Griffith continued. "The doctor told us that when they brought you out of the mine, you were dripping with water. He said you had even had a little water in your airway. All the years I've been in Bethell, the mine has never flooded. I've never heard of water in the mine. And one more thing," the Father reached into a pocket in his coat and removed something. "The doctor also gave us this."

He placed a small pouch into Matthew's hand. From the expression on Matthew's face both the father and the bishop knew Matthew recognized the item. "The doctor said you had this gripped in your right hand. Matthew, what happened? Did you have another uh . . . trip?"

Matthew stared at the two for a moment then answered, "Yes."

"Was it as before, to the birthplace?" asked Griffith.

"No," replied Matthew. "It was at the resurrection. I was a Roman soldier guarding the tomb."

The bishop spoke up, "Matthew, please start with the last thing you remember in the mine until you awoke here in the hospital. Don't leave a thing out."

Matthew nodded. He started by telling them about finding the trapped miners, his foot becoming caught, and finally the ceiling falling in. How it was becoming difficult to breathe from all of the dust, and everything going black. He hesitated. Father Griffith urged him to continue. Matthew launched into his experience.

Matthew talked for several hours, with the bishop and Father Griffith totally focused on every detail of his description. Neither said a word while Matthew explained every activity, sound, smell, and thought he had. Finally, Matthew described his attack and subsequent drowning.

He held up the pouch Father Griffith had handed him. "This is the item I pulled from the neck of my attacker." Matthew loosened the leather cord holding the pouch closed and dumped the contents onto his bed next to him. Matthew smiled. "This is similar to some of the coins we were given by the Sanhedrin to perpetuate their story about the grave being robbed."

Matthew handed a few of the coins to Father Griffith, who passed a couple to Mayweather. They all examined the coins, turning them over. Some of the coins were pristine, like they were minted yesterday. Others were worn, nicked, and bent. One of the ones Father Griffith held even had a tooth mark where one of its previous owners had checked its worth by biting it.

Bishop Mayweather pondered, "In my earlier days, I did a brief study in the Smithsonian in Roman antiquities. This coin," holding up one that looked like it was silver, "is a denarius, a Roman coin. And this is a drachma, a Greek coin. And this slightly worn one is a Jewish coin called a beka. These three coins represent four days' wages at the time of Christ, if I'm remembering my coinage correctly. Even this beka is in far better condition than I have ever seen."

"Most of these look freshly minted," remarked Father Griffith. "Some of the markings would disappear with minor wear." Father Griffith started replacing the coins in the pouch. He collected the coins from the bishop and from Matthew and placed them into the pouch.

As Father Griffith tightened the cord around the pouch, closing it, he started to hand it to Matthew.

"Please, Father Griffith," requested Matthew. "Would you hold on to the pouch for me? I've been told I'm not going anywhere for the next few days."

"Certainly," complied Father Griffith.

"But there is one thing I've missed," started Matthew.

"Ah, let me guess," said the bishop as he got up out of his chair and went back around the screen. A moment later, he returned carrying Matthew's shepherd's crook. "A man named Pappy presented this to us while we were on our way over here. He said you would be wanting it."

Father Griffith added, "Pappy said it was resting by the mine entrance, where the miners register their badges before going underground."

"I was afraid something might happen to it down there, and I didn't have a card to leave showing I had gone down," said Matthew. "I must thank Pappy for bringing it over."

The bishop walked to the other side of Matthew's bed and rested the crook up against the wall. "This seems to be a proper place for your crook," he said thoughtfully.

Matthew thanked him as the bishop moved back to his chair. As he sat down the doctor joined the party. "Gentlemen," said the doctor announcing himself, "I've come to check on my patient. Matthew, how are you feeling?"

"I'm doing fine," replied Matthew. "I've been behaving myself, just been talking."

"Good, but you're starting to look a little tired. Have you rested any today?"

"I've just been sitting here, talking," Matthew said with a smile.

"Yes, I see," mused the doctor. "It's a few hours before dinner. I'd like for you to have a little rest before Mrs. Johnston brings your meal."

"The Father and I fully understand," inserted the bishop. "I would like to know how long it will be before Father Matthew is able to travel."

The doctor looked a little surprised. "It's a little early to say. I want his ankle to heal a little more before putting any weight on it. Then there will be a period of rehabilitation." The bishop looked quizzically at the doctor. "At least two weeks, and it could be four weeks depending on the ankle."

"Very good," replied the bishop. "Father Griffith and I need to make a few phone calls."

Father Griffith looked surprised. "Who do we need to call?"

"We need to call to get a replacement for this parish. And we'll need to make travel arrangements for the three of us."

"But bishop, I thought I would be covering things here while Father Matthew convalesced." said Father Griffith.

"Your time here was already determined. And Father Matthew will have difficulty traveling in this country. Besides, I think there are other things that need to be investigated here," said the bishop as he turned his focus on Matthew. "Come, Father Griffith. Matthew needs to rest, and we have phone calls to make."

"Doctor, can I come back and visit Matthew in the early evening?" asked Father Griffith.

The doctor nodded, "A short visit after dinner will be fine."

"Thank you, doctor," replied Father Griffith. "Matthew, I'll be back later. Do what the doctor says."

"Come, Father," said Mayweather. The two stepped around the screen, and their foot falls faded away.

"All right, Matthew, time to rest. Would you like some assistance lying back?" asked the doctor.

Matthew started to try and shift himself to lay back, but the pillows hindered his movement. "I think I could use a little assistance."

The doctor smirked, started to pull out a pillow or two, and helped ease Matthew back into a lying position. "How's that? Do you need anything for the pain?"

"This is fine. And the pain is not bad." replied Matthew.

"All right. If you need anything, just call out. Either Mrs. Johnston or I will be close by. Get some rest."

Matthew settled in. As he lay there, he started thinking about what the bishop had said, but before there was much contemplation, Matthew dosed off.

# EPILOGUE

A little over two months had passed. But here he was, standing in the middle of St. John's Cathedral. Even though it was roughly nineteen months ago that he had been told he would be going to Bethell instead of a cathedral, it seemed a lifetime ago. Standing there, leaning on his shepherd's crook, Matthew surveyed the grand surroundings. The stone work, hand-hewn woodwork, and stained-glass windows surrounded him with awestriking grandeur. And yet, Matthew found no comfort or desire for this setting. The craftsmanship was inspiring, but it was not what God would want.

It screamed "man." He was sure that some of the individuals who crafted these minor miracles did them out of devotion. But the architects were interested in their legacy, something for others to remember them by. So, this is what he had been so upset with just prior leaving from school. He felt ashamed for the way he had acted. And yet, he realized that there was something else. The two events he had had the privilege to witness, the birth and then the resurrection, were both in humble settings. Yet, these were events meant for people, everyday common people.

God was providing a way for a person to find his way through life, back to his creator. And yet, man had taken these events and turned them into so many different denominations, so many religions. Matthew's train of thought was broken by a slight twinge of pain from his ankle. He shifted his weight to the other foot and his crook to get some relief.

Matthew thought about the last several weeks of rehabilitation to re-gain his strength and learn how to walk on his twisted foot. Matthew shifted his weight while leaning on his crook to try to rest the damaged ankle. He remembered the bishop telling him that there were others he needed to tell his "stories" to. Father Griffith seemed to be uneasy with this prospect.

At one point when the two were briefly alone, Father Griffith had told Matthew, "Stay true to your experiences. They are gifts. For what purpose, I do not know." These moments with Father Griffith were rare, since Bishop Mayweather always seemed to be present.

Matthew also thought it strange that when their replacement arrived, Father Williams, only a few days were spent performing the changeover. Matthew thought it would at least take a month to make the transition. And the doctor didn't seem to be too happy with Mayweather when he insisted that they travel as soon as possible. Matthew overheard the doctor and Mayweather discussing the plans that the bishop had for getting Matthew to this cathedral.

The doctor kept urging Mayweather not to have Matthew travel for another couple of weeks. He also wanted to make arrangements for Matthew to see a surgeon at the city's main hospital. Matthew remembered Mayweather telling the doctor that church business came first, but that he would guarantee that Matthew would see a surgeon as soon as other matters were handled. Those "other matters" had concerned Matthew. So, he asked the bishop what "other matters" were.

The bishop told Matthew it was nothing to be concerned with. They were standard reports that needed to be done, especially since Matthew had been directly involved in the mine cave-in. This seemed to have a ring of truth, but Mayweather seemed to be more interested in Matthew's "experiences" when he first arrived in Bethell and after he had lost consciousness in the mine. Several times, while Matthew was recovering, Mayweather had Matthew retell his experiences.

During one of these sessions, Mayweather seemed to be confused about details in Matthew's stories. Several times, Matthew had to reexplain and correct some of the details that the bishop would repeat with errors. Matthew felt that the bishop was testing him. At the end of that particular session, the bishop seemed to be very pleased.

Matthew reached into the pocket of his pants and felt the pouch containing the coins. He realized for the first time he was at peace with himself. He felt as though he had been struggling all of his life to find something, his purpose, his place in life. He felt as though he had arrived. He wasn't sure where that was, but it felt right. At the same time, Matthew noticed one of the stained-glass windows, high up in one of the cathedral's walls. The sunlight backlit the window, causing the colors to spill across the floor. The rich reds, blues, greens, and yellows washed the stone floor with colors.

As Matthew studied the window's artwork, he realized the scene was that of the burial tomb with a roman soldier laying at the base and two people kneeling on either side of the entrance. Above the door was Christ in his risen glory. The round stone to seal the tomb looked small and frail compared to what Matthew had remembered.

But the one question that had been a constant companion ever since he arrived in Bethell was *Why me?* He had had the privilege of being witness to two of the greatest times in human history. Why? He glanced back to the window.

"Why?" he whispered.

A sound of someone approaching pulled his attention from the window scene. "Father," said the young man. "The council is ready to meet with you."

Matthew stared at the young man for a moment. Matthew guessed that they were close to the same age, but felt like he was half again as old as this young priest. Matthew nodded and returned his gaze to the window.

"Father, please follow me. The council . . ."

Matthew thought out loud, "Very, very close, but not quite right," while still looking at the window.

"Father?" The young man motioned back the way he had come.

Matthew turned to the young man. "Yes, please lead on."

The two left the cathedral, heading toward a side door. When they reached the door, the young man held it open for Matthew to enter. Matthew hesitated for a moment, turned, and glanced one more time at the colorful window. The sunlight still illuminated the window. He gave a little grin as he shook his head, turned, and passed through the door with the aid of his crook.

The young priest followed Matthew and closed the door behind himself, leaving a soft thud of the closing door to echo in the empty cathedral.

www.ingramcontent.com/pod-product-compliance
Lightning Source LLC
Chambersburg PA
CBHW050406030726
47503CB00006B/2047